D1505573

STONE ARCH BOOKS
a capstone imprint

STONE ARCH BOOKS™

Published in 2014 by Stone Arch Books
A Capstone Imprint
1710 Roe Crest Drive
North Mankato, MN 56003
www.capstonepub.com

Originally published by DC Comics in the U.S. in single
magazine form as Batman: Li'l Gotham.
Copyright © 2014 DC Comics. All Rights Reserved.

DC Comics
1700 Broadway, New York, NY 10019
A Warner Bros. Entertainment Company
No part of this publication may be reproduced in whole
or in part, or stored in a retrieval system, or transmitted
in any form or by any means, electronic, mechanical,
photocopying, recording, or otherwise, without written
permission.

Printed in China.
032014   008085LEOF14

Cataloging-in-Publication Data is available at the Library
of Congress website:
ISBN: 978-1-4342-9208-7 (library binding)

Summary: On Halloween night, will Robin be able to tell
the difference between all the costumed children and
the real evildoers, or will the kids get clobbered while
the villains escape?! Then, on Thanksgiving, Batman and
Robin join the families of Gotham in gathering around
the table for a big holiday turkey...until another flightless fowl shows up--the Penguin!

STONE ARCH BOOKS
Ashley C. Andersen Zantop **Publisher**
Michael Dahl **Editorial Director**
Sean Tulien **Editor**
Heather Kindseth **Creative Director**
Bob Lentz **Art Director**
Hilary Wacholz **Designer**
Kathy McColley **Production Specialist**

DC Comics
Sarah Gaydos **Original U.S. Editor**

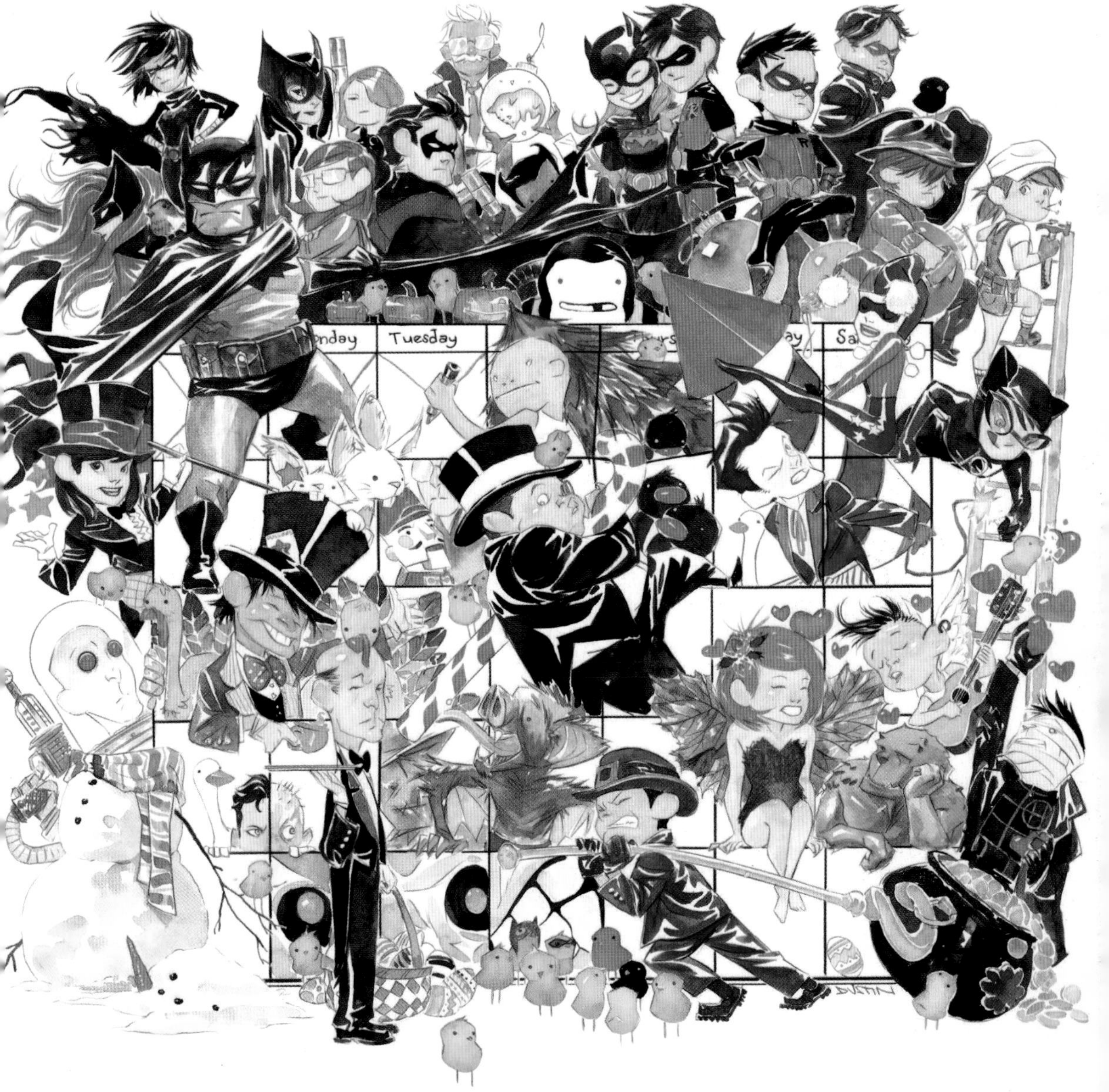
Tuesday
DUSTIN

HALLOWEEN AND THANKSGIVING

Dustin Nguyen & Derek Fridolfs....................... writers
Dustin Nguyen... artist
Saida Temofonte... letterer

BATMAN created by
Bob Kane

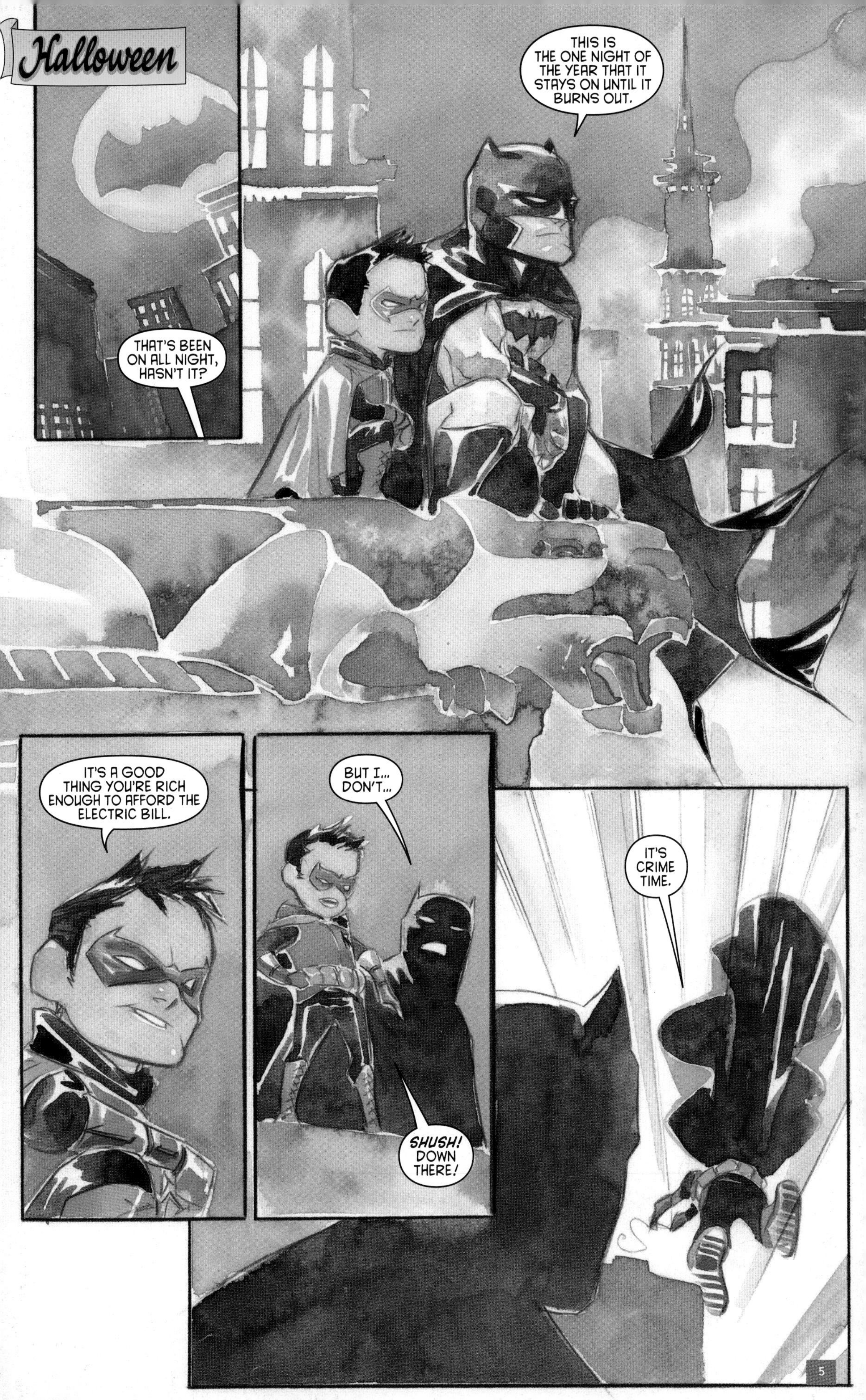
Halloween
THAT'S BEEN ON ALL NIGHT, HASN'T IT?
THIS IS THE ONE NIGHT OF THE YEAR THAT IT STAYS ON UNTIL IT BURNS OUT.
IT'S A GOOD THING YOU'RE RICH ENOUGH TO AFFORD THE ELECTRIC BILL.
BUT I... DON'T...
SHUSH! DOWN THERE!
IT'S CRIME TIME.

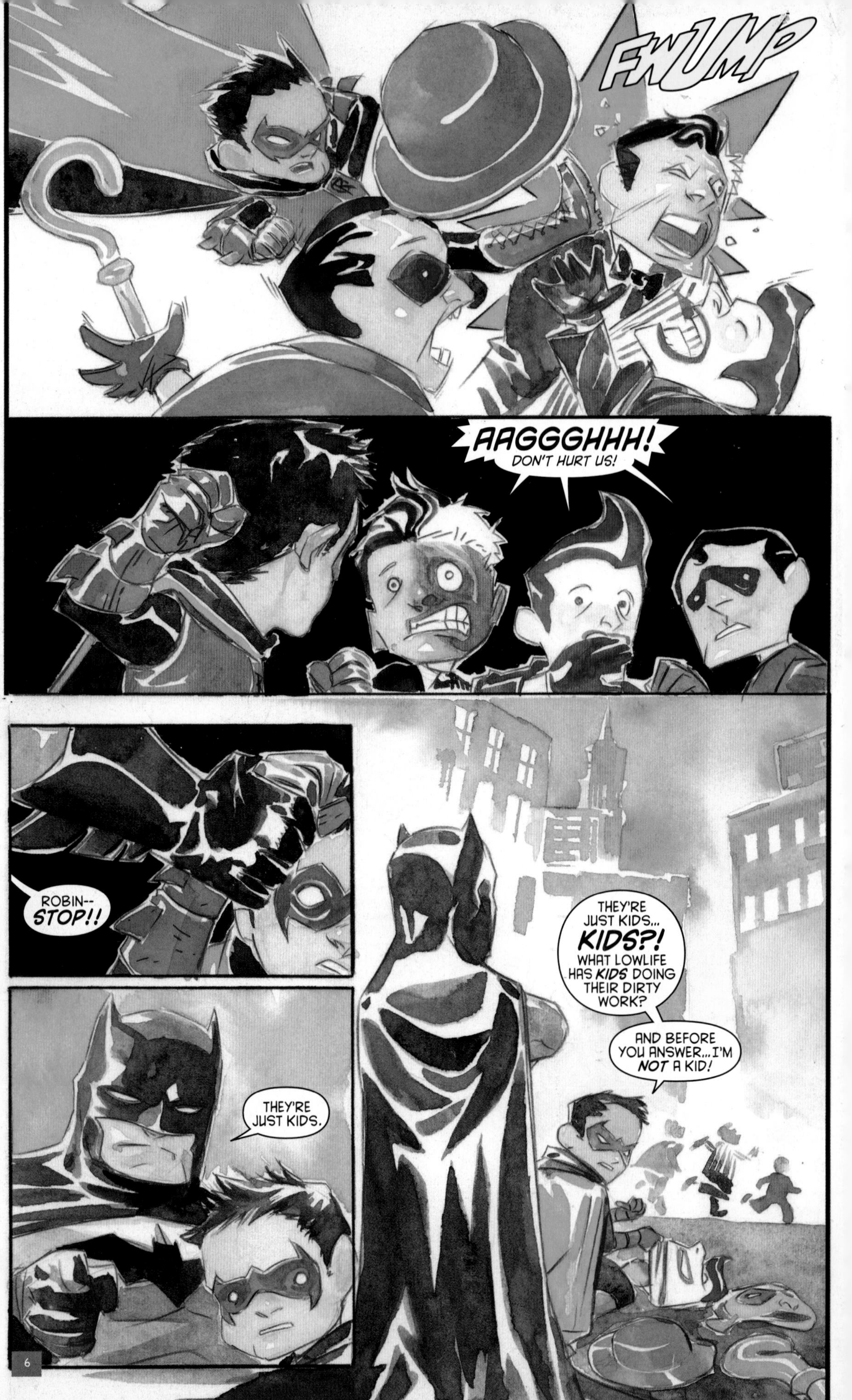
FWUMP
AAGGGHHH!
DON'T HURT US!
ROBIN--
STOP!!
THEY'RE
JUST KIDS.
THEY'RE
JUST KIDS...
KIDS?!
WHAT LOWLIFE
HAS KIDS DOING
THEIR DIRTY
WORK?
AND BEFORE
YOU ANSWER...I'M
NOT A KID!

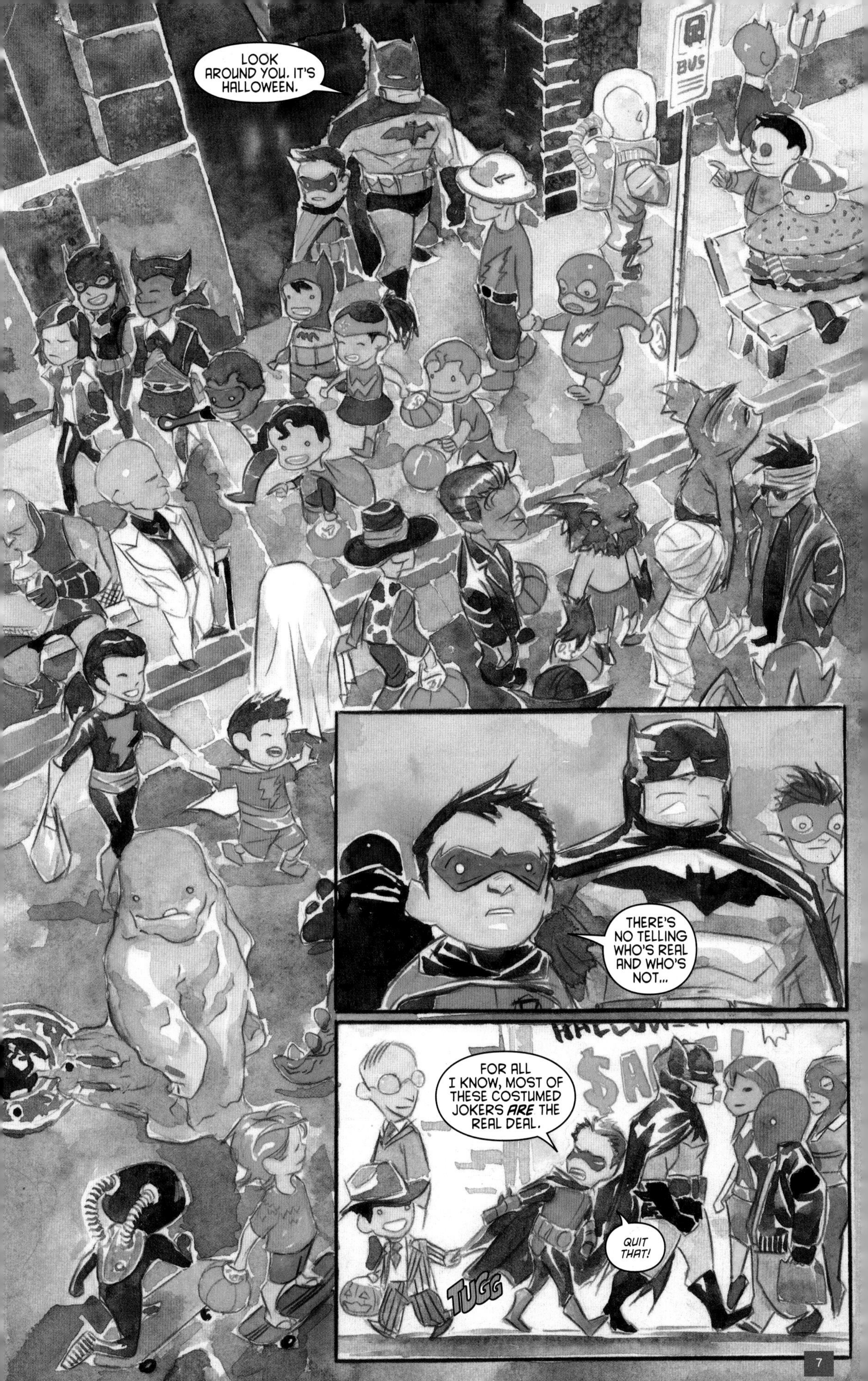
LOOK AROUND YOU. IT'S HALLOWEEN.
BUS
THERE'S NO TELLING WHO'S REAL AND WHO'S NOT...
FOR ALL I KNOW, MOST OF THESE COSTUMED JOKERS *ARE* THE REAL DEAL.
TUGG
QUIT THAT!

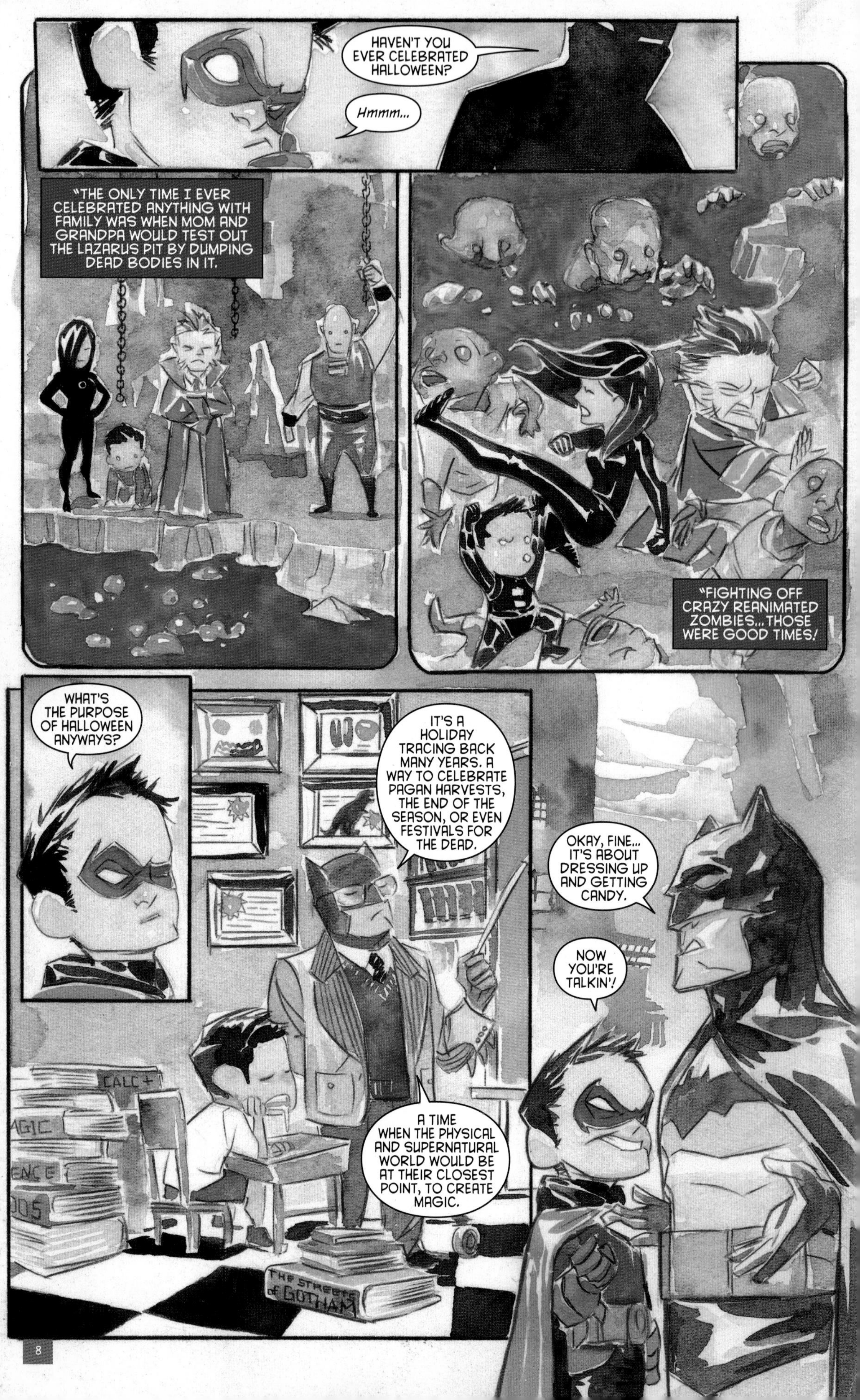
HAVEN'T YOU EVER CELEBRATED HALLOWEEN?
Hmmm...
"THE ONLY TIME I EVER CELEBRATED ANYTHING WITH FAMILY WAS WHEN MOM AND GRANDPA WOULD TEST OUT THE LAZARUS PIT BY DUMPING DEAD BODIES IN IT.
"FIGHTING OFF CRAZY REANIMATED ZOMBIES... THOSE WERE GOOD TIMES!
WHAT'S THE PURPOSE OF HALLOWEEN ANYWAYS?
IT'S A HOLIDAY TRACING BACK MANY YEARS. A WAY TO CELEBRATE PAGAN HARVESTS, THE END OF THE SEASON, OR EVEN FESTIVALS FOR THE DEAD.
A TIME WHEN THE PHYSICAL AND SUPERNATURAL WORLD WOULD BE AT THEIR CLOSEST POINT, TO CREATE MAGIC.
OKAY, FINE... IT'S ABOUT DRESSING UP AND GETTING CANDY.
NOW YOU'RE TALKIN'!
CALC+
THE STREETS OF GOTHAM

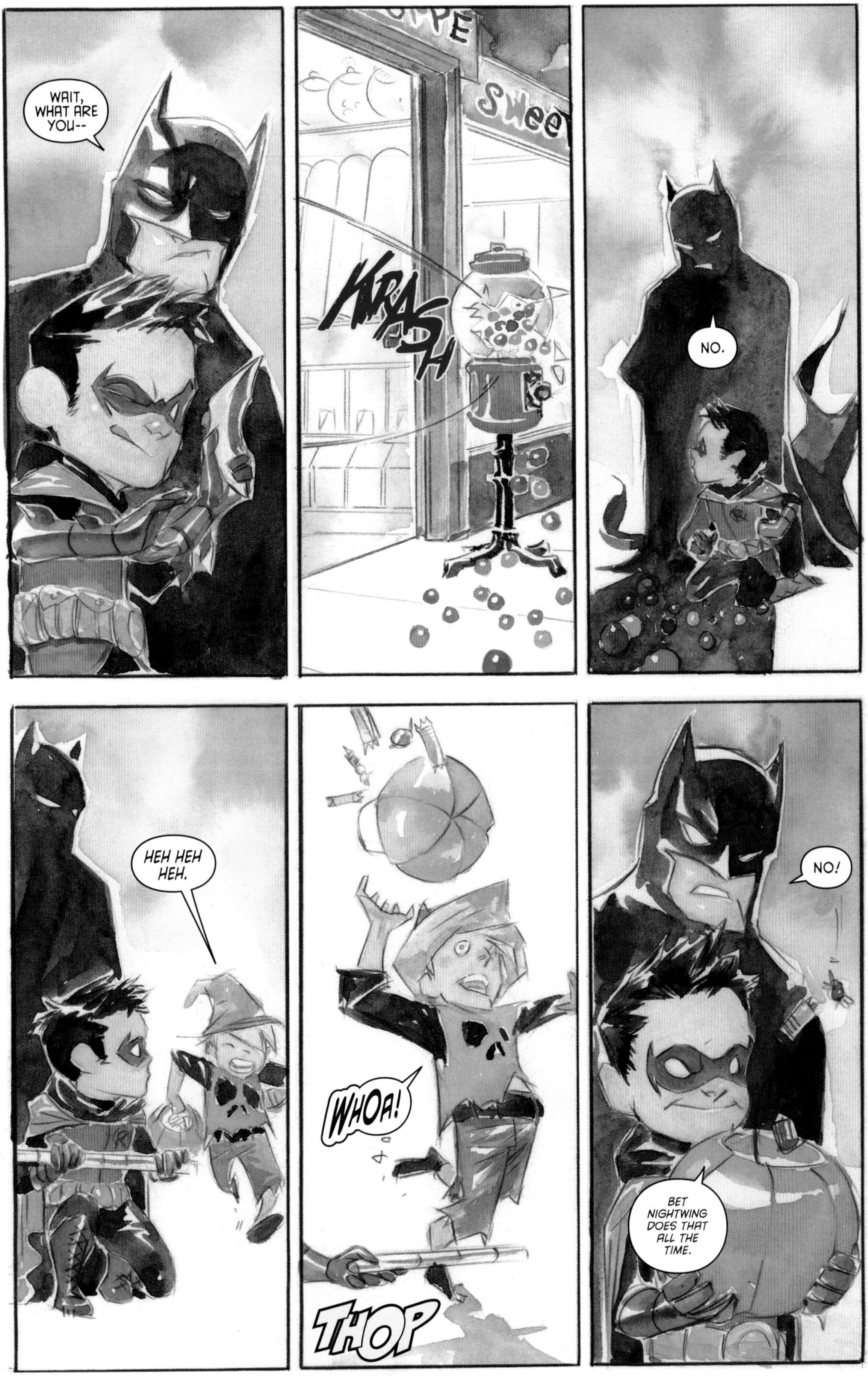
WAIT, WHAT ARE YOU--
SWEET
KRASH
NO.
HEH HEH HEH.
WHOA!
THOP
NO!
BET NIGHTWING DOES THAT ALL THE TIME.

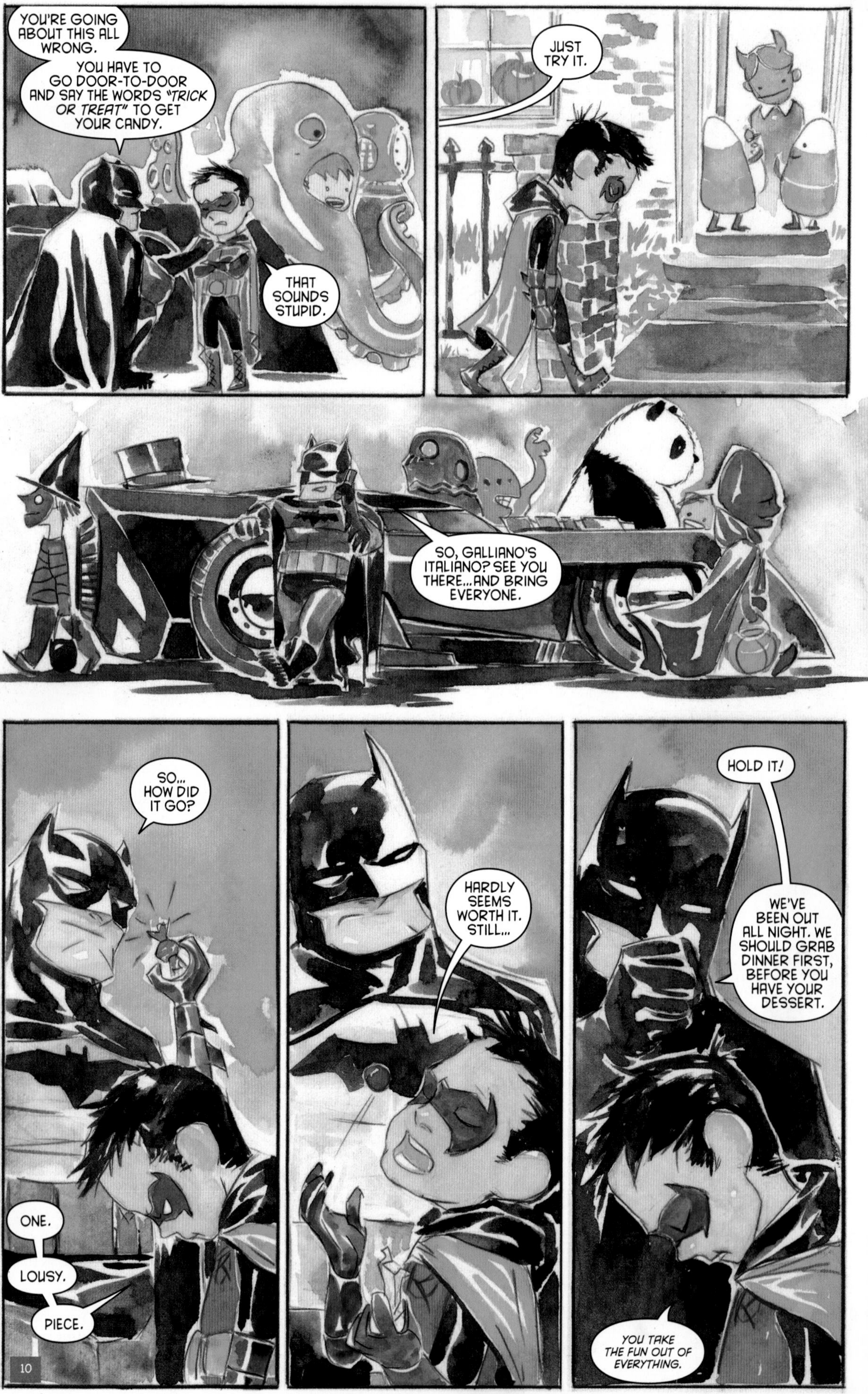

YOU'RE GOING ABOUT THIS ALL WRONG.
YOU HAVE TO GO DOOR-TO-DOOR AND SAY THE WORDS *"TRICK OR TREAT"* TO GET YOUR CANDY.
THAT SOUNDS STUPID.
JUST TRY IT.
SO, GALLIANO'S ITALIANO? SEE YOU THERE...AND BRING EVERYONE.
SO... HOW DID IT GO?
ONE.
LOUSY.
PIECE.
HARDLY SEEMS WORTH IT. STILL...
HOLD IT!
WE'VE BEEN OUT ALL NIGHT. WE SHOULD GRAB DINNER FIRST, BEFORE YOU HAVE YOUR DESSERT.
YOU TAKE THE FUN OUT OF EVERYTHING.

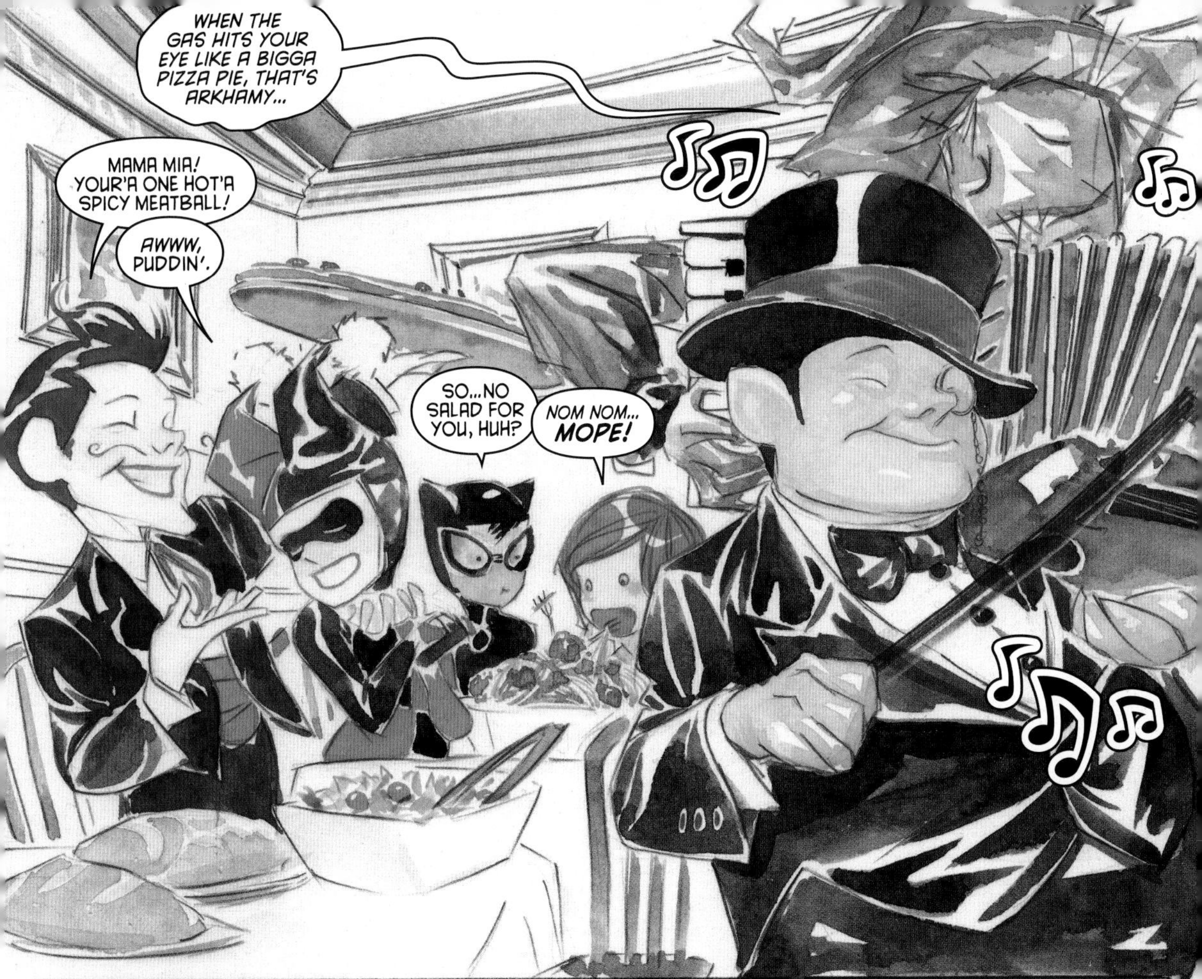
WHEN THE GAS HITS YOUR EYE LIKE A BIGGA PIZZA PIE, THAT'S ARKHAMY...
MAMA MIA! YOUR'A ONE HOT'A SPICY MEATBALL!
AWWW, PUDDIN'.
SO...NO SALAD FOR YOU, HUH?
NOM NOM... MOPE!

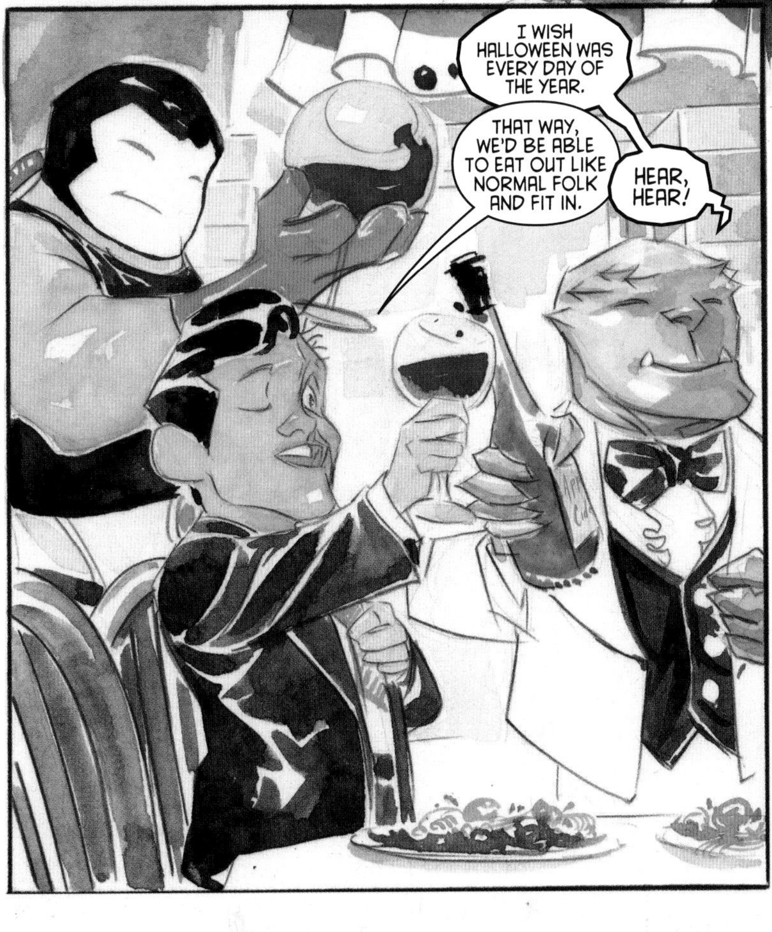
I WISH HALLOWEEN WAS EVERY DAY OF THE YEAR.
THAT WAY, WE'D BE ABLE TO EAT OUT LIKE NORMAL FOLK AND FIT IN.
HEAR, HEAR!

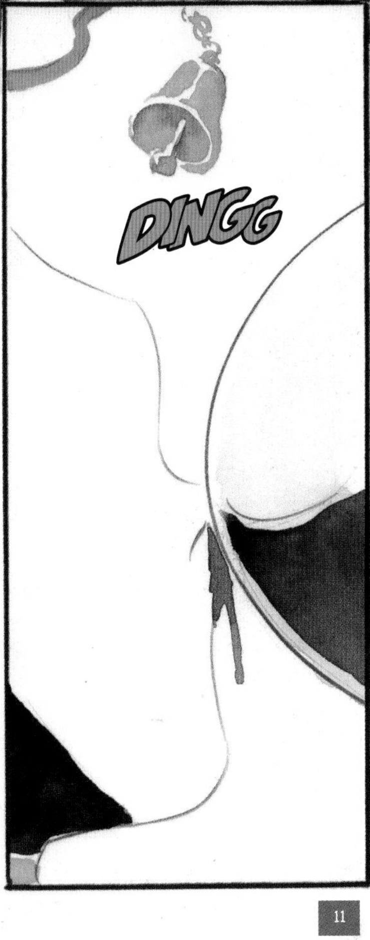
DINGG

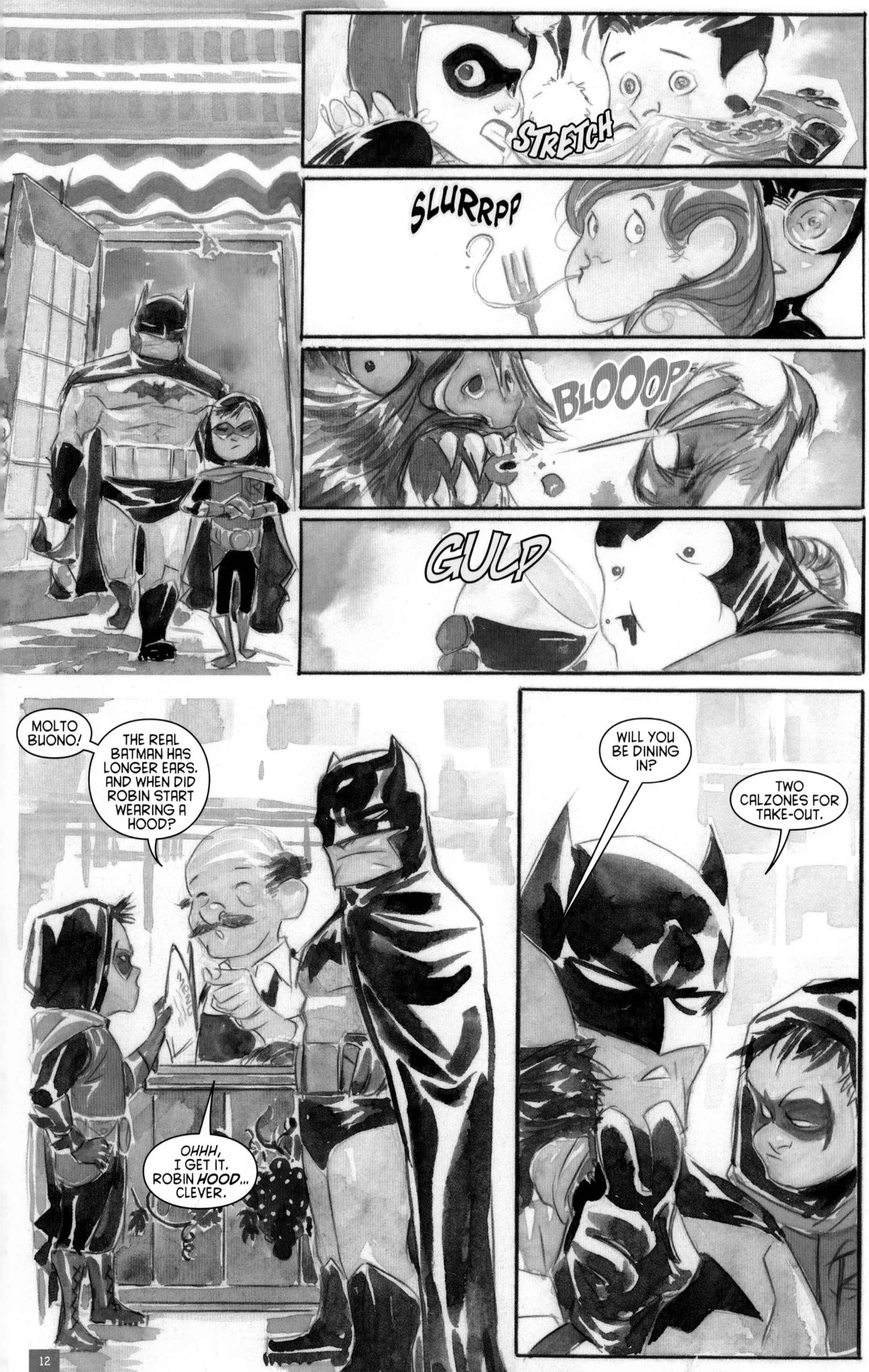
STRETCH
SLURRPP
BLOOOP
GULP
MOLTO BUONO!
THE REAL BATMAN HAS LONGER EARS. AND WHEN DID ROBIN START WEARING A HOOD?
OHHH, I GET IT. ROBIN HOOD... CLEVER.
WILL YOU BE DINING IN?
TWO CALZONES FOR TAKE-OUT.

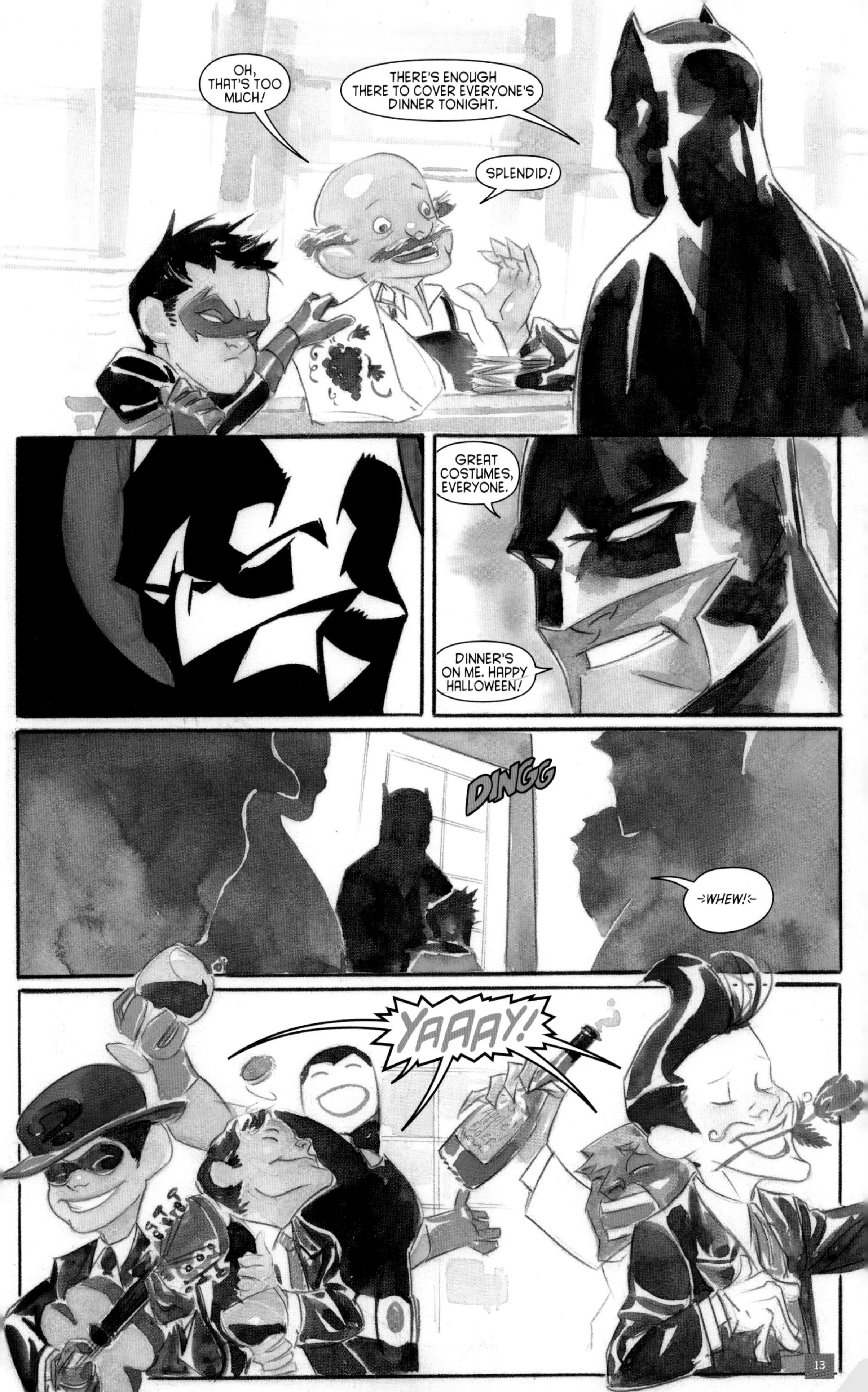
OH, THAT'S TOO MUCH!
THERE'S ENOUGH THERE TO COVER EVERYONE'S DINNER TONIGHT.
SPLENDID!
GREAT COSTUMES, EVERYONE.
DINNER'S ON ME. HAPPY HALLOWEEN!
DINGG
WHEW!
YAAAY!

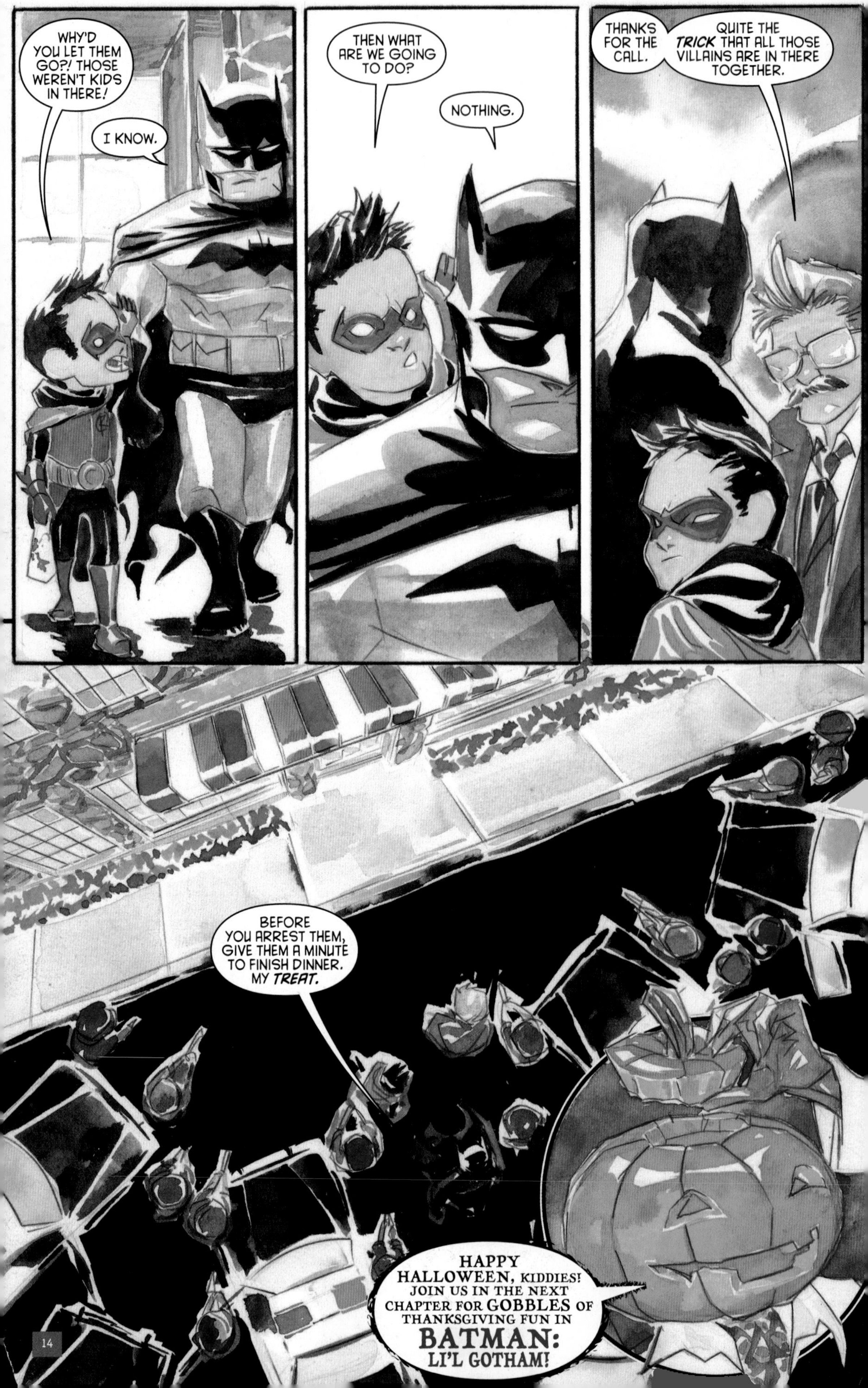
WHY'D YOU LET THEM GO?! THOSE WEREN'T KIDS IN THERE!
I KNOW.
THEN WHAT ARE WE GOING TO DO?
NOTHING.
THANKS FOR THE CALL.
QUITE THE *TRICK* THAT ALL THOSE VILLAINS ARE IN THERE TOGETHER.
BEFORE YOU ARREST THEM, GIVE THEM A MINUTE TO FINISH DINNER. MY *TREAT.*
HAPPY HALLOWEEN, KIDDIES! JOIN US IN THE NEXT CHAPTER FOR GOBBLES OF THANKSGIVING FUN IN BATMAN: LI'L GOTHAM!

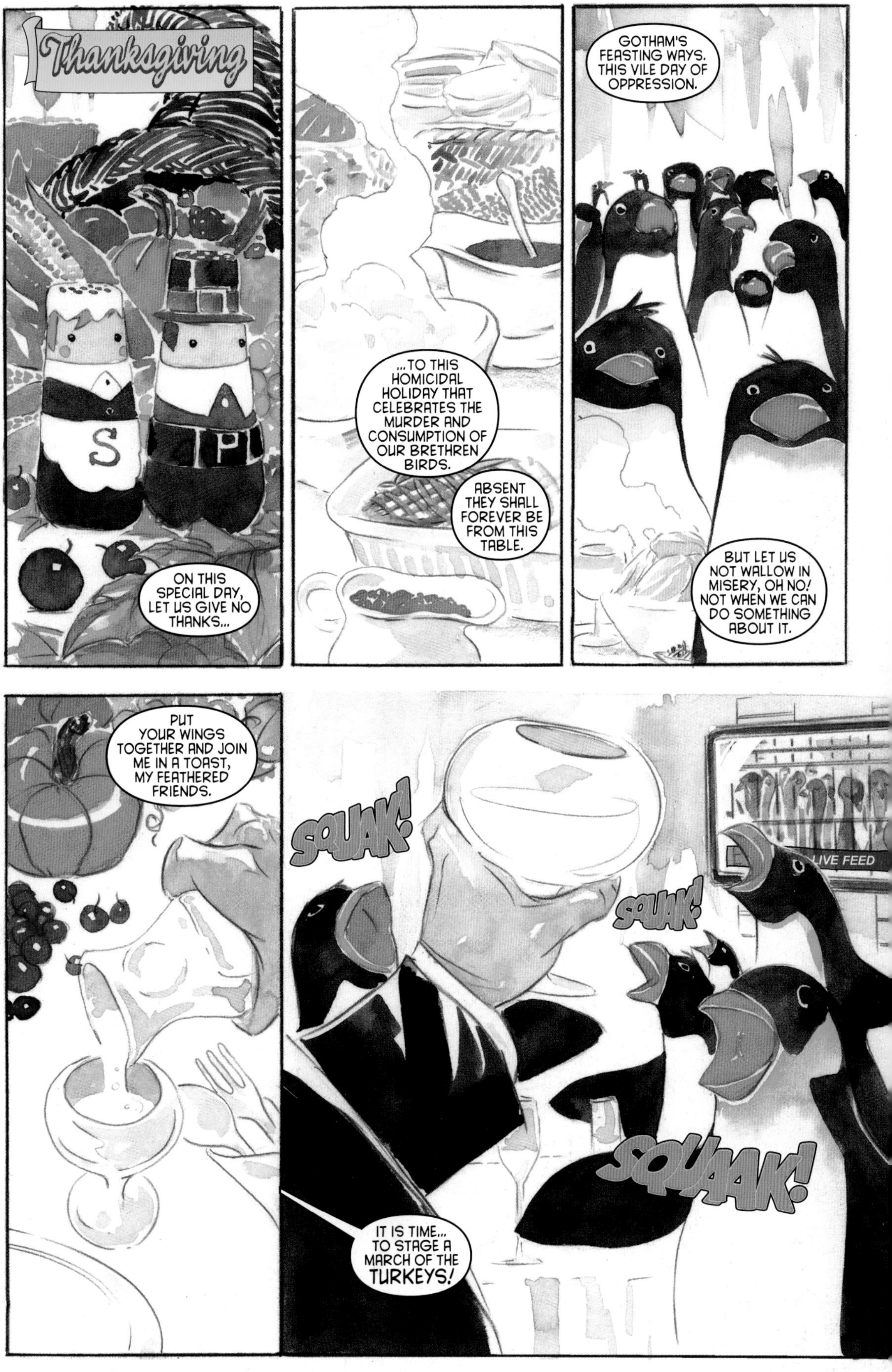
Thanksgiving
ON THIS SPECIAL DAY, LET US GIVE NO THANKS...
...TO THIS HOMICIDAL HOLIDAY THAT CELEBRATES THE MURDER AND CONSUMPTION OF OUR BRETHREN BIRDS.
ABSENT THEY SHALL FOREVER BE FROM THIS TABLE.
GOTHAM'S FEASTING WAYS. THIS VILE DAY OF OPPRESSION.
BUT LET US NOT WALLOW IN MISERY, OH NO! NOT WHEN WE CAN DO SOMETHING ABOUT IT.
PUT YOUR WINGS TOGETHER AND JOIN ME IN A TOAST, MY FEATHERED FRIENDS.
SQUAK!
LIVE FEED
SQUAK!
SQUAAK!
IT IS TIME... TO STAGE A MARCH OF THE TURKEYS!

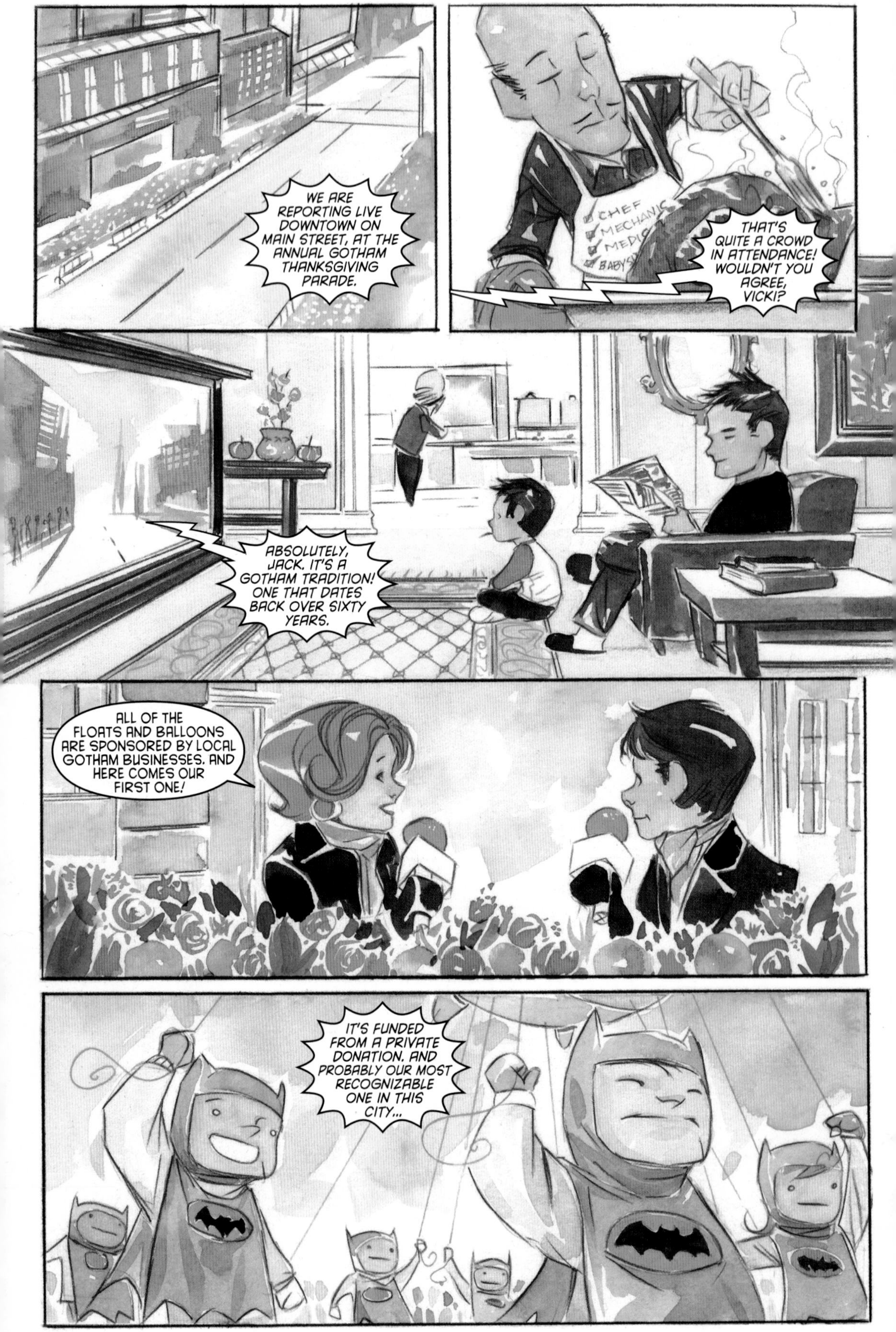
WE ARE REPORTING LIVE DOWNTOWN ON MAIN STREET, AT THE ANNUAL GOTHAM THANKSGIVING PARADE.
CHEF
MECHANIC
THAT'S QUITE A CROWD IN ATTENDANCE! WOULDN'T YOU AGREE, VICKI?
ABSOLUTELY, JACK. IT'S A GOTHAM TRADITION! ONE THAT DATES BACK OVER SIXTY YEARS.
ALL OF THE FLOATS AND BALLOONS ARE SPONSORED BY LOCAL GOTHAM BUSINESSES. AND HERE COMES OUR FIRST ONE!
IT'S FUNDED FROM A PRIVATE DONATION. AND PROBABLY OUR MOST RECOGNIZABLE ONE IN THIS CITY...

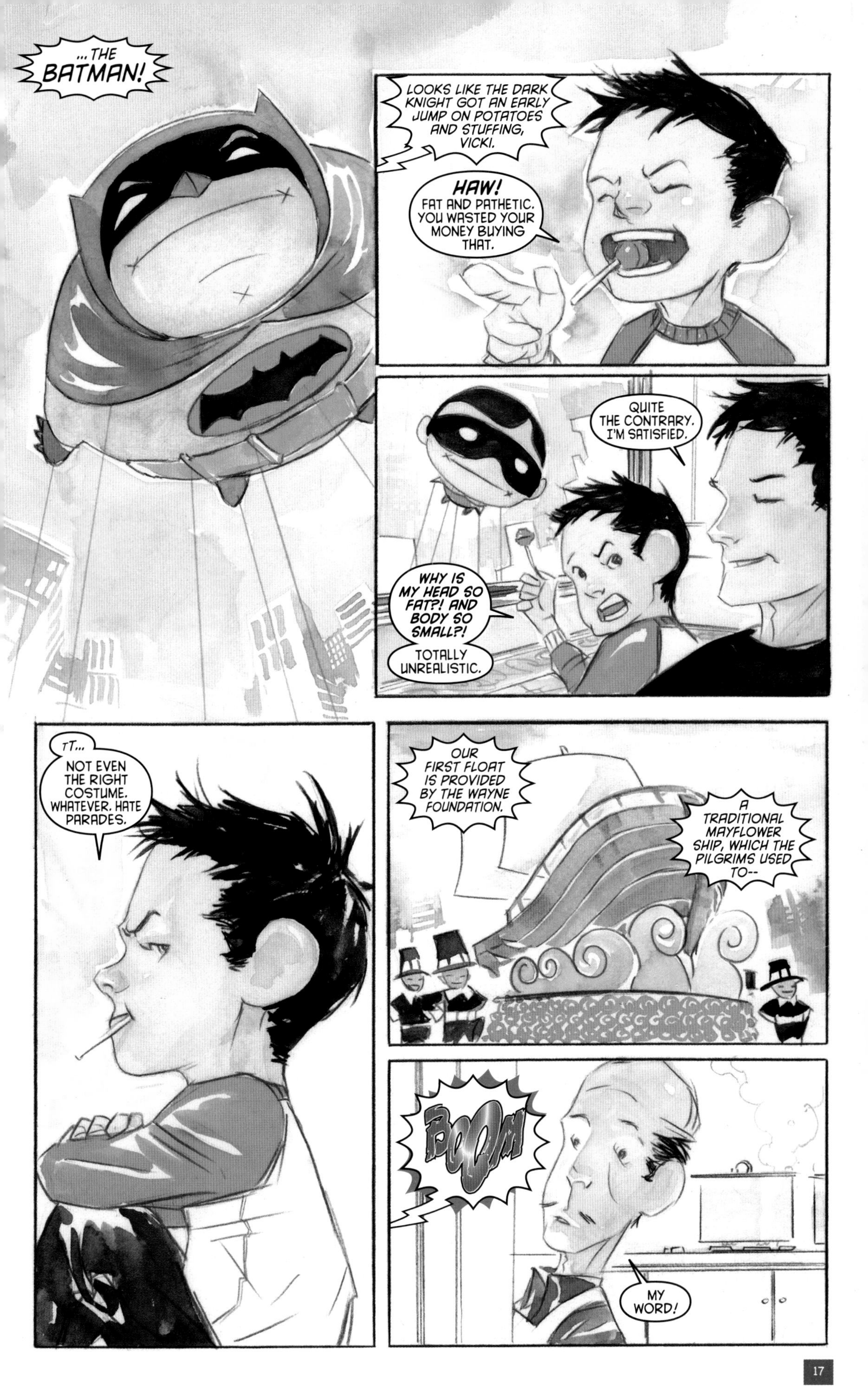
...THE BATMAN!
LOOKS LIKE THE DARK KNIGHT GOT AN EARLY JUMP ON POTATOES AND STUFFING, VICKI.
HAW! FAT AND PATHETIC. YOU WASTED YOUR MONEY BUYING THAT.
QUITE THE CONTRARY. I'M SATISFIED.
WHY IS MY HEAD SO FAT?! AND BODY SO SMALL?!
TOTALLY UNREALISTIC.
TT...
NOT EVEN THE RIGHT COSTUME. WHATEVER. HATE PARADES.
OUR FIRST FLOAT IS PROVIDED BY THE WAYNE FOUNDATION.
A TRADITIONAL MAYFLOWER SHIP, WHICH THE PILGRIMS USED TO--
BOOM
MY WORD!

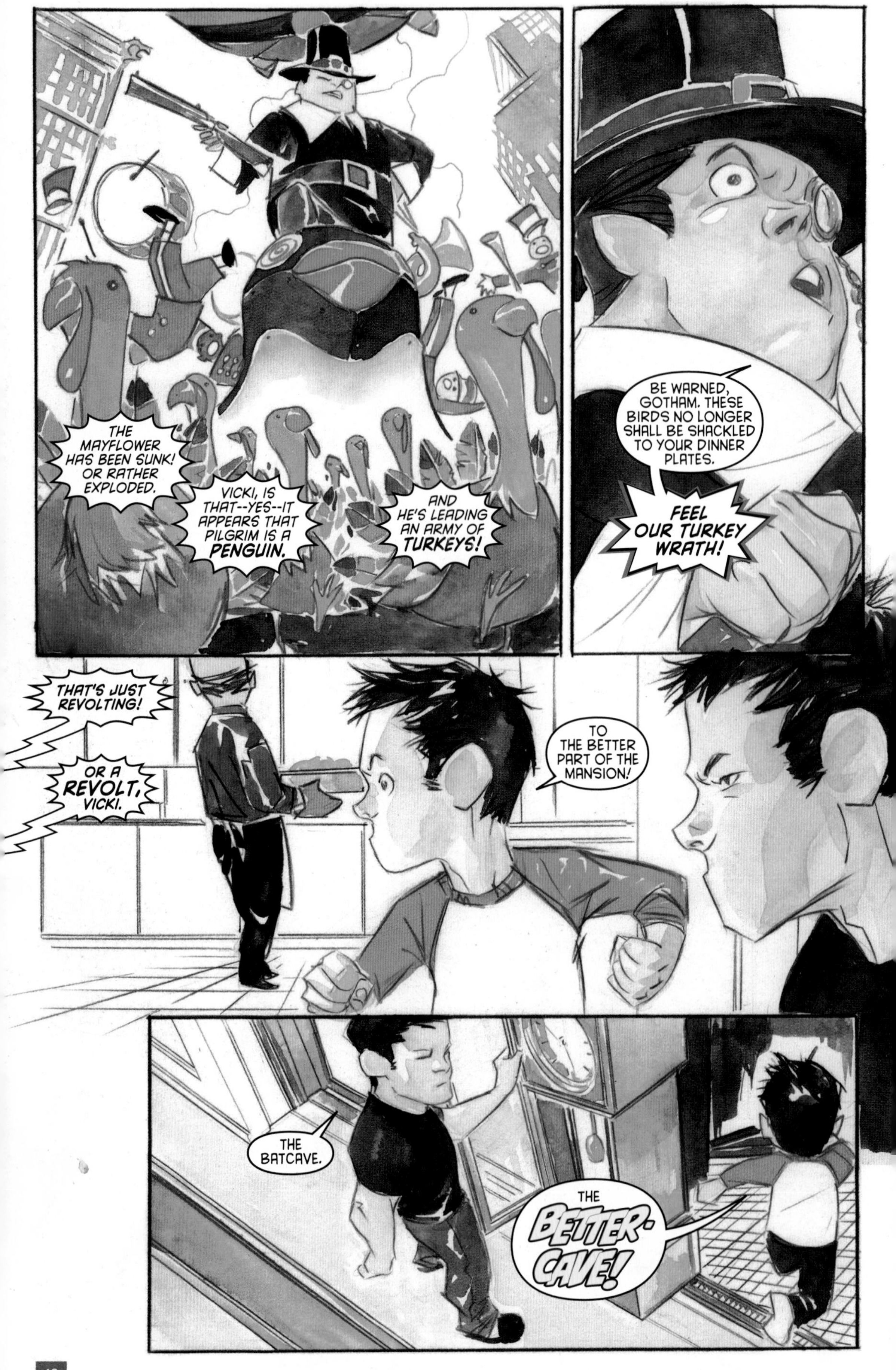
THE MAYFLOWER HAS BEEN SUNK! OR RATHER EXPLODED.
VICKI, IS THAT--YES--IT APPEARS THAT PILGRIM IS A PENGUIN.
AND HE'S LEADING AN ARMY OF TURKEYS!
BE WARNED, GOTHAM. THESE BIRDS NO LONGER SHALL BE SHACKLED TO YOUR DINNER PLATES.
FEEL OUR TURKEY WRATH!
THAT'S JUST REVOLTING!
OR A REVOLT, VICKI.
TO THE BETTER PART OF THE MANSION!
THE BATCAVE.
THE BETTER-CAVE!

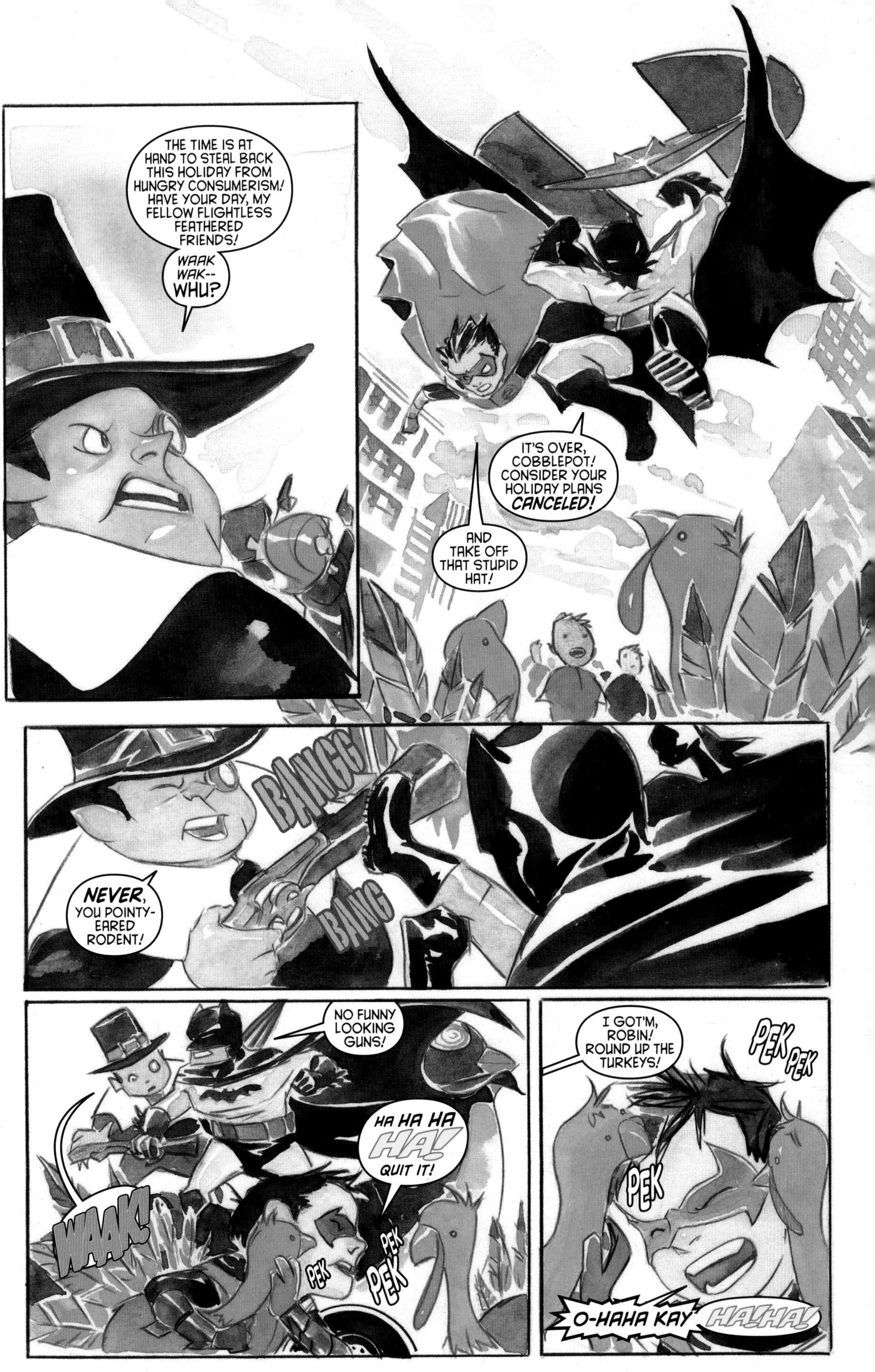
THE TIME IS AT HAND TO STEAL BACK THIS HOLIDAY FROM HUNGRY CONSUMERISM! HAVE YOUR DAY, MY FELLOW FLIGHTLESS FEATHERED FRIENDS!
WAAK WAK-- WHU?
IT'S OVER, COBBLEPOT! CONSIDER YOUR HOLIDAY PLANS CANCELED!
AND TAKE OFF THAT STUPID HAT!
BANGG
BANG
NEVER, YOU POINTY-EARED RODENT!
NO FUNNY LOOKING GUNS!
HA HA HA HA! QUIT IT!
WAAK!
PEK
PEK PEK
I GOT'M, ROBIN! ROUND UP THE TURKEYS!
PEK PEK
PEK
O-HAHA KAY HA!HA!

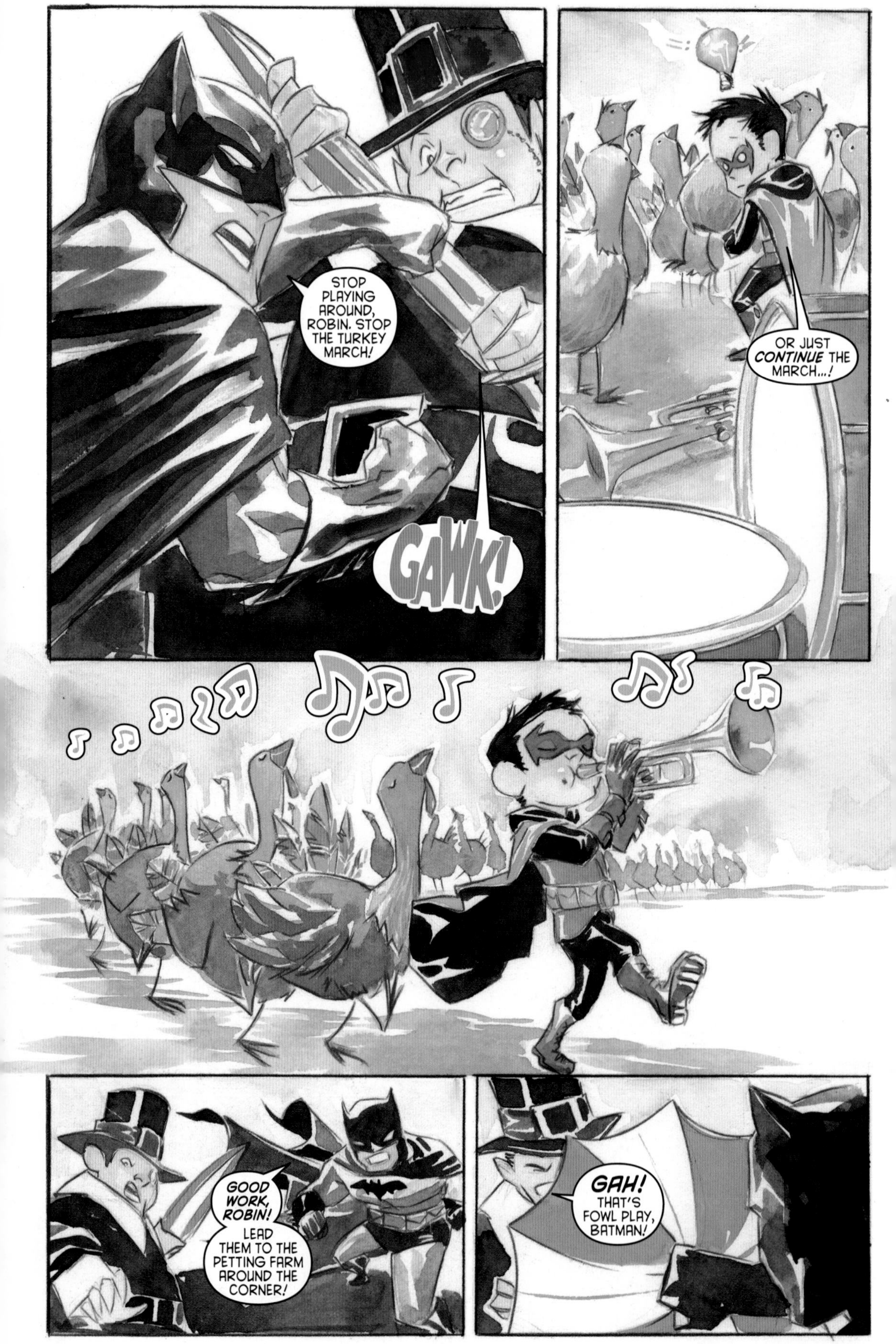
STOP PLAYING AROUND, ROBIN. STOP THE TURKEY MARCH!
GAWK!
OR JUST *CONTINUE* THE MARCH...!
GOOD WORK, ROBIN!
LEAD THEM TO THE PETTING FARM AROUND THE CORNER!
GAH! THAT'S FOWL PLAY, BATMAN!

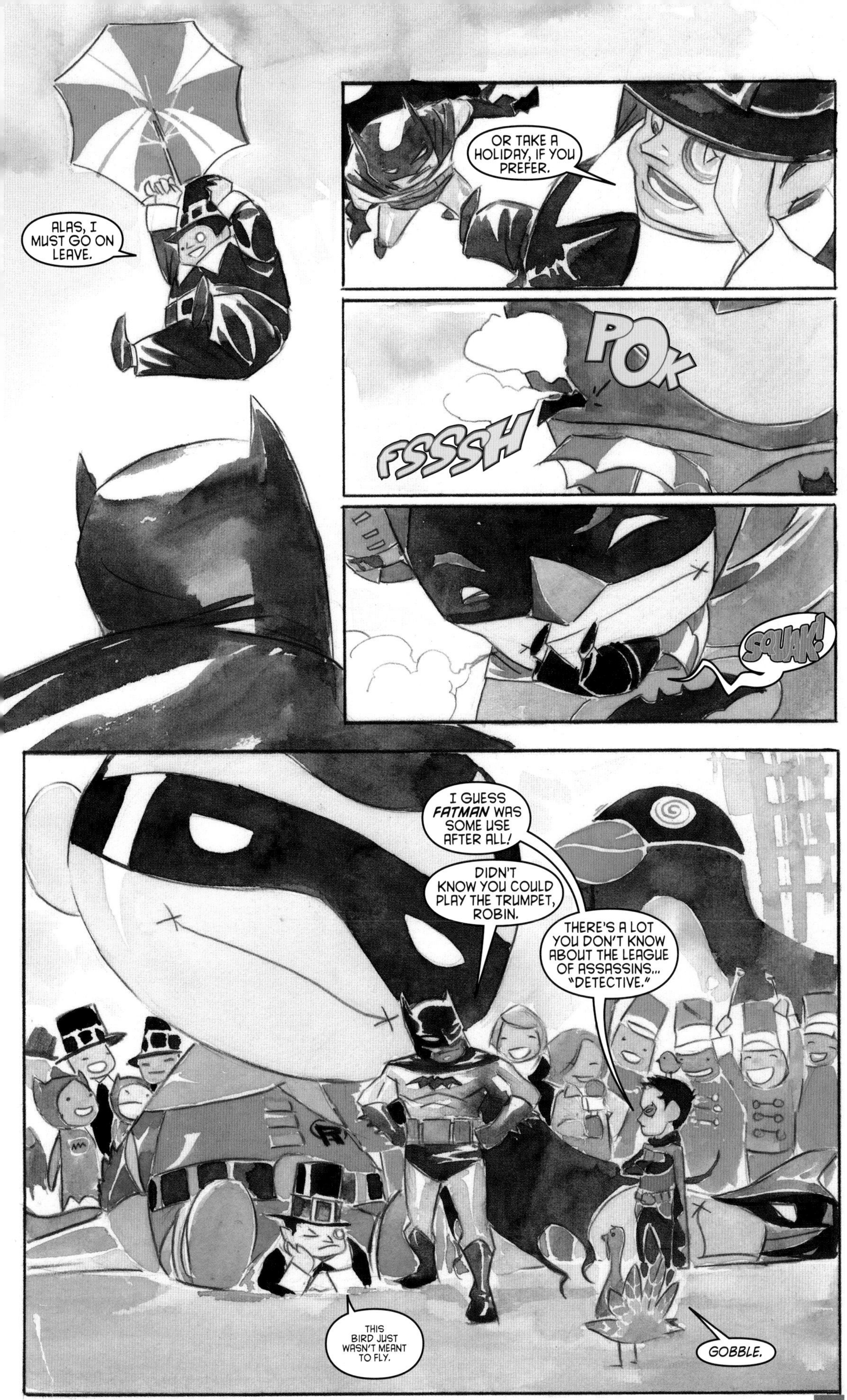
ALAS, I MUST GO ON LEAVE.
OR TAKE A HOLIDAY, IF YOU PREFER.
POK
FSSSH
SQUAK!
I GUESS *FATMAN* WAS SOME USE AFTER ALL!
DIDN'T KNOW YOU COULD PLAY THE TRUMPET, ROBIN.
THERE'S A LOT YOU DON'T KNOW ABOUT THE LEAGUE OF ASSASSINS... "DETECTIVE."
THIS BIRD JUST WASN'T MEANT TO FLY.
GOBBLE.

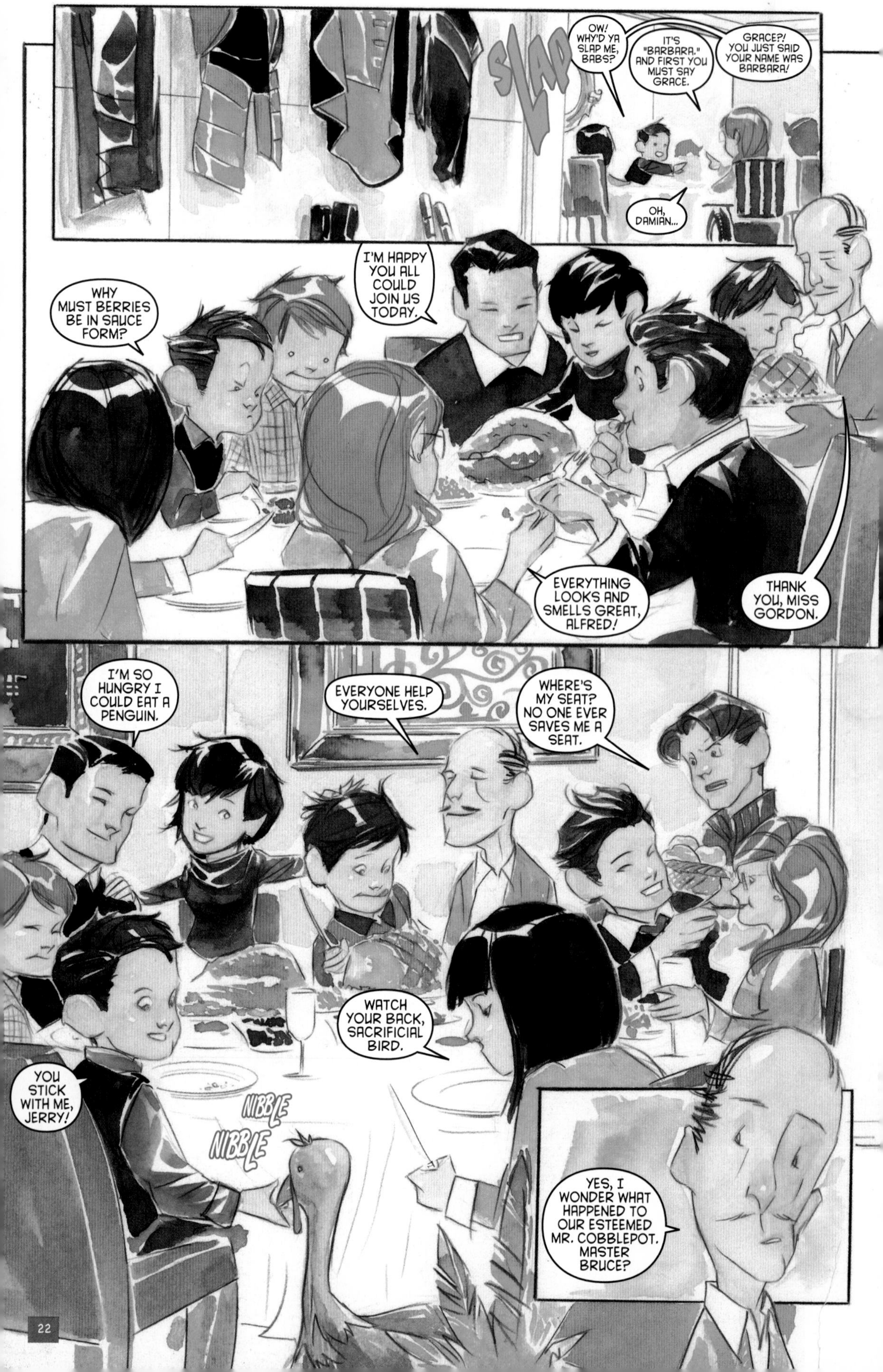
SLAP
OW! WHY'D YA SLAP ME, BABS?
IT'S "BARBARA." AND FIRST YOU MUST SAY GRACE.
GRACE?! YOU JUST SAID YOUR NAME WAS BARBARA!
OH, DAMIAN...
WHY MUST BERRIES BE IN SAUCE FORM?
I'M HAPPY YOU ALL COULD JOIN US TODAY.
EVERYTHING LOOKS AND SMELLS GREAT, ALFRED!
THANK YOU, MISS GORDON.
I'M SO HUNGRY I COULD EAT A PENGUIN.
EVERYONE HELP YOURSELVES.
WHERE'S MY SEAT? NO ONE EVER SAVES ME A SEAT.
WATCH YOUR BACK, SACRIFICIAL BIRD.
YOU STICK WITH ME, JERRY!
NIBBLE
NIBBLE
YES, I WONDER WHAT HAPPENED TO OUR ESTEEMED MR. COBBLEPOT. MASTER BRUCE?

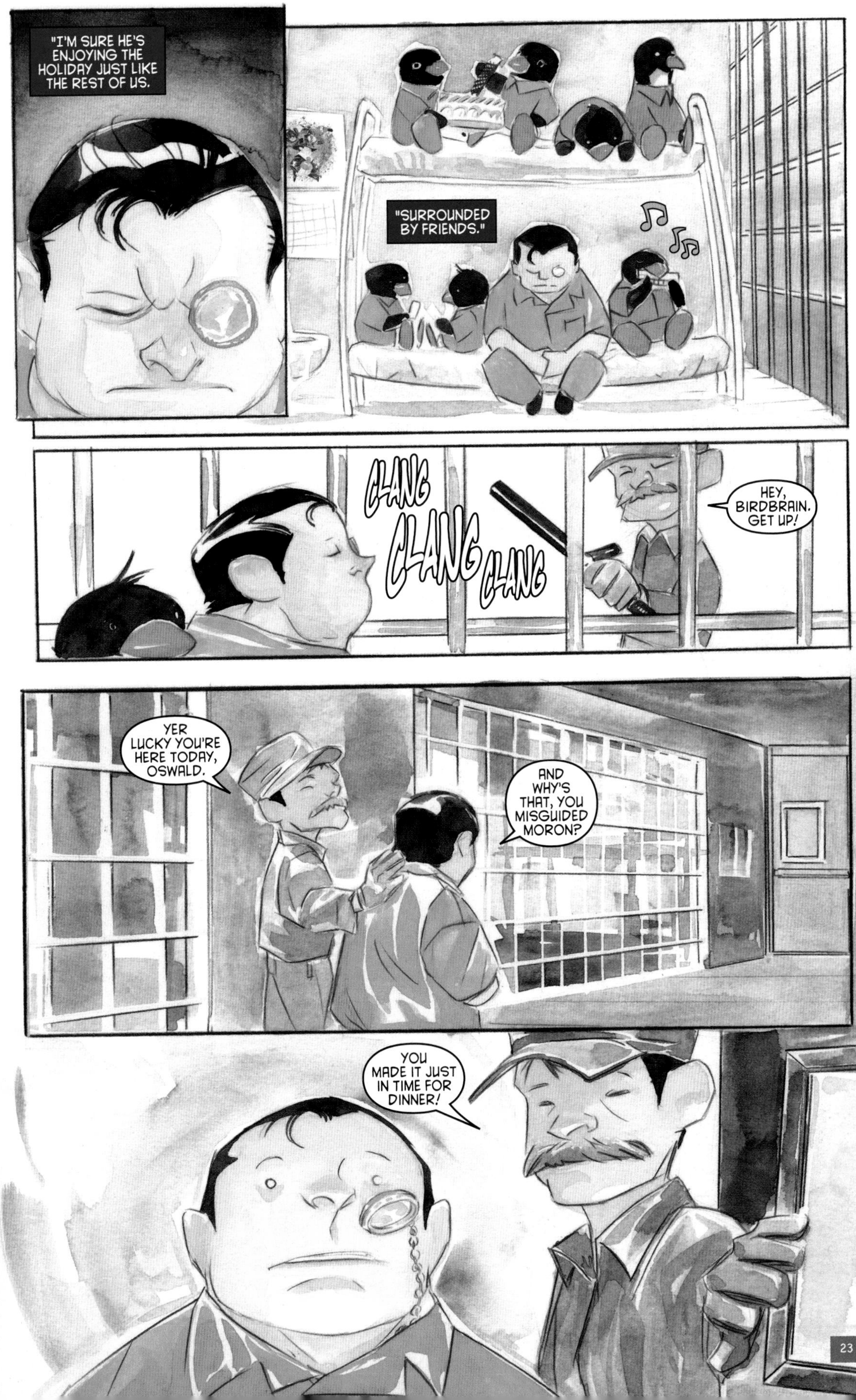
"I'M SURE HE'S ENJOYING THE HOLIDAY JUST LIKE THE REST OF US.
"SURROUNDED BY FRIENDS."
CLANG CLANG CLANG
HEY, BIRDBRAIN. GET UP!
YER LUCKY YOU'RE HERE TODAY, OSWALD.
AND WHY'S THAT, YOU MISGUIDED MORON?
YOU MADE IT JUST IN TIME FOR DINNER!

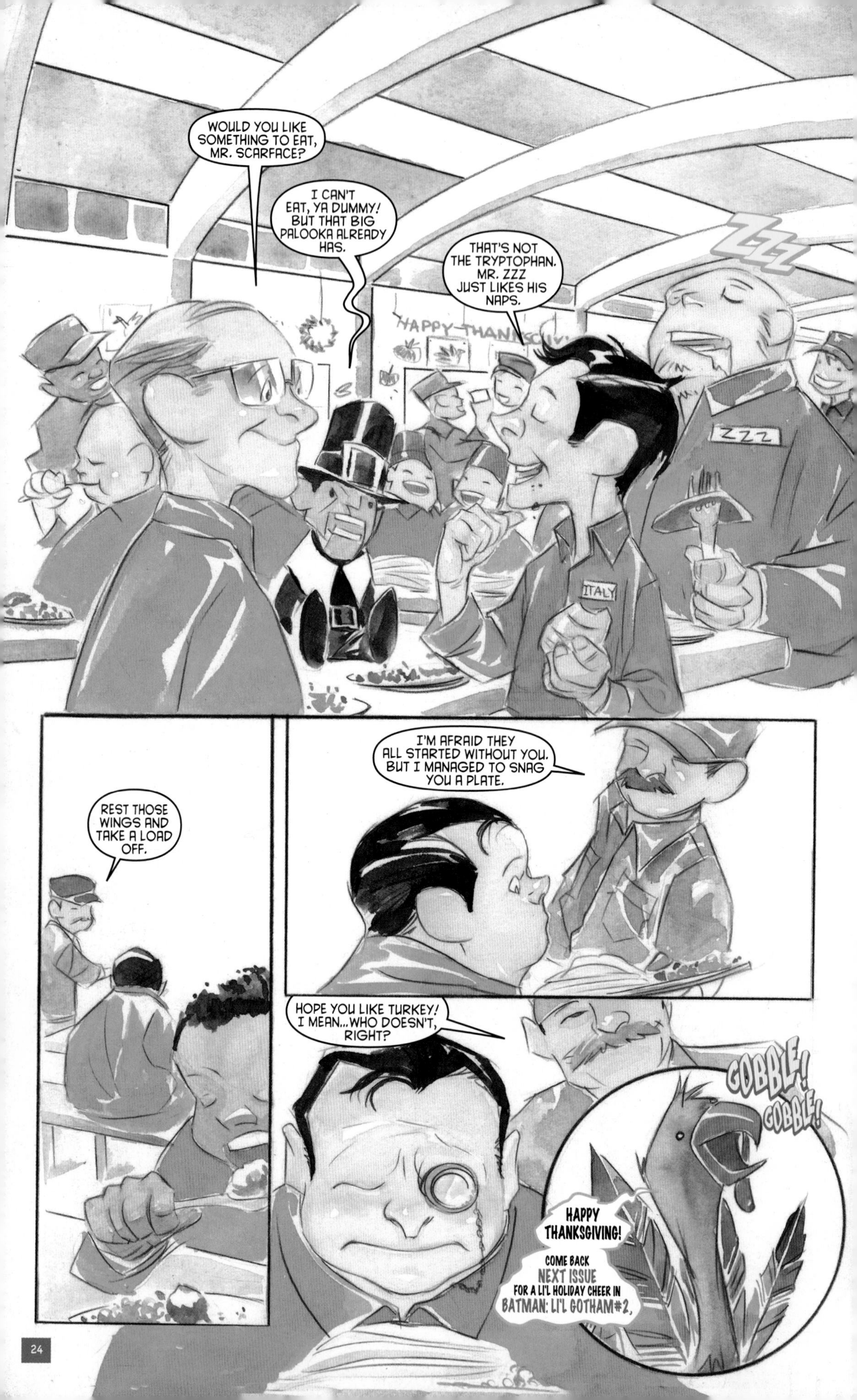
WOULD YOU LIKE SOMETHING TO EAT, MR. SCARFACE?
I CAN'T EAT, YA DUMMY! BUT THAT BIG PALOOKA ALREADY HAS.
THAT'S NOT THE TRYPTOPHAN. MR. ZZZ JUST LIKES HIS NAPS.
ZZZ
ZZZ
ITALY
REST THOSE WINGS AND TAKE A LOAD OFF.
I'M AFRAID THEY ALL STARTED WITHOUT YOU. BUT I MANAGED TO SNAG YOU A PLATE.
HOPE YOU LIKE TURKEY! I MEAN...WHO DOESN'T, RIGHT?
GOBBLE! GOBBLE!
HAPPY THANKSGIVING!
COME BACK NEXT ISSUE FOR A LI'L HOLIDAY CHEER IN BATMAN: LI'L GOTHAM #2,

CREATORS

DUSTIN NGUYEN — CO-WRITER & ILLUSTRATOR

Dustin Nguyen is an American comic artist whose body of work includes Wildcats v3.0, The Authority Revolution, Batman, Superman/Batman, Detective Comics, Batgirl, and his creator owned project Manifest Eternity. Currently, he produces all the art for Batman: Li'l Gotham, which is also written by himself and Derek Fridolfs. Outside of comics, Dustin moonlights as a conceptual artist for toys, games, and animation. In his spare time, he enjoys sleeping, driving, and sketching things he loves.

DEREK FRIDOLFS — CO-WRITER

Derek Fridolfs is a comic book writer, inker, and artist. He resides in Gotham--present and future.

GLOSSARY

festivals (FESS-tuh-vuhls)--days or times of celebration that are marked by feasting, ceremonies, or other traditions

Lazarus Pit (LAZZ-er-uhss PITZ)--a mysterious fluid-filled pit in the earth that regenerates and even revives the dead or dying. The lazarus pit is used by the League of Assassins, which Damian a.k.a. Robin used to be a member of.

misery (MIZ-er-ee)--great sadness or distress

pagan (PAY-guhn)--a follower of a polytheistic religion (a religion that has more than one god)

harvest (HAR-vest)--the season when crops are gathered from the fields, or the activity of gathering crops

oppression (oh-PREH-shuhn)--cruel or unjust use of authority or power

reanimated (re-AN-uh-may-tid)--returned to life

revolt (re-VOLT)--to rise up against the authority of a ruler or government, or to feel disgust or shock

supernatural (soo-per-NAT-chur-uhl)--beyond the visible or observable world we live in

vile (VYLE)--very bad or ugly

VISUAL QUESTIONS & PROMPTS

1. Both Robin and the Penguin have their own animal armies in this book. If you could have an army of your own, what animal would you choose? Why?

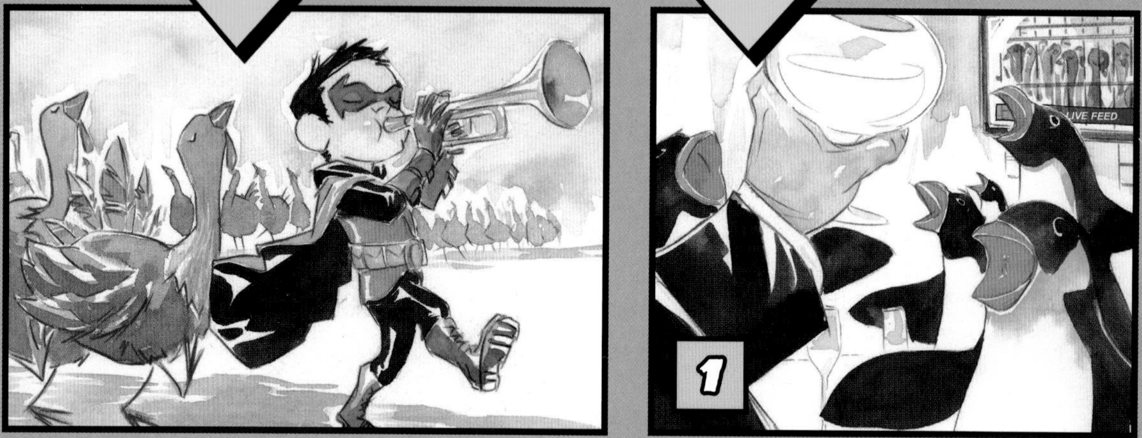
LIVE FEED
1

2. Based on the panel below (and the other panels on page 8, what do you think the Lazarus Pits are used for? Why?

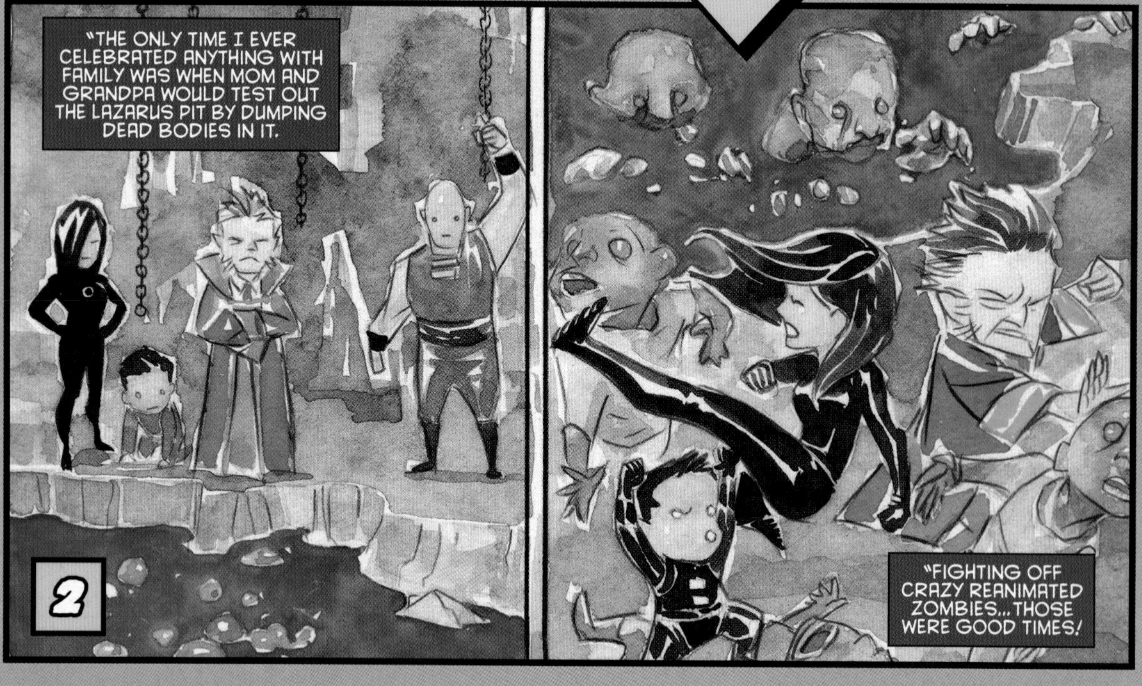
"THE ONLY TIME I EVER CELEBRATED ANYTHING WITH FAMILY WAS WHEN MOM AND GRANDPA WOULD TEST OUT THE LAZARUS PIT BY DUMPING DEAD BODIES IN IT.
2
"FIGHTING OFF CRAZY REANIMATED ZOMBIES... THOSE WERE GOOD TIMES!

3. Why would having so many people in costumes make fighting crime difficult? Think up as many reasons as you can.

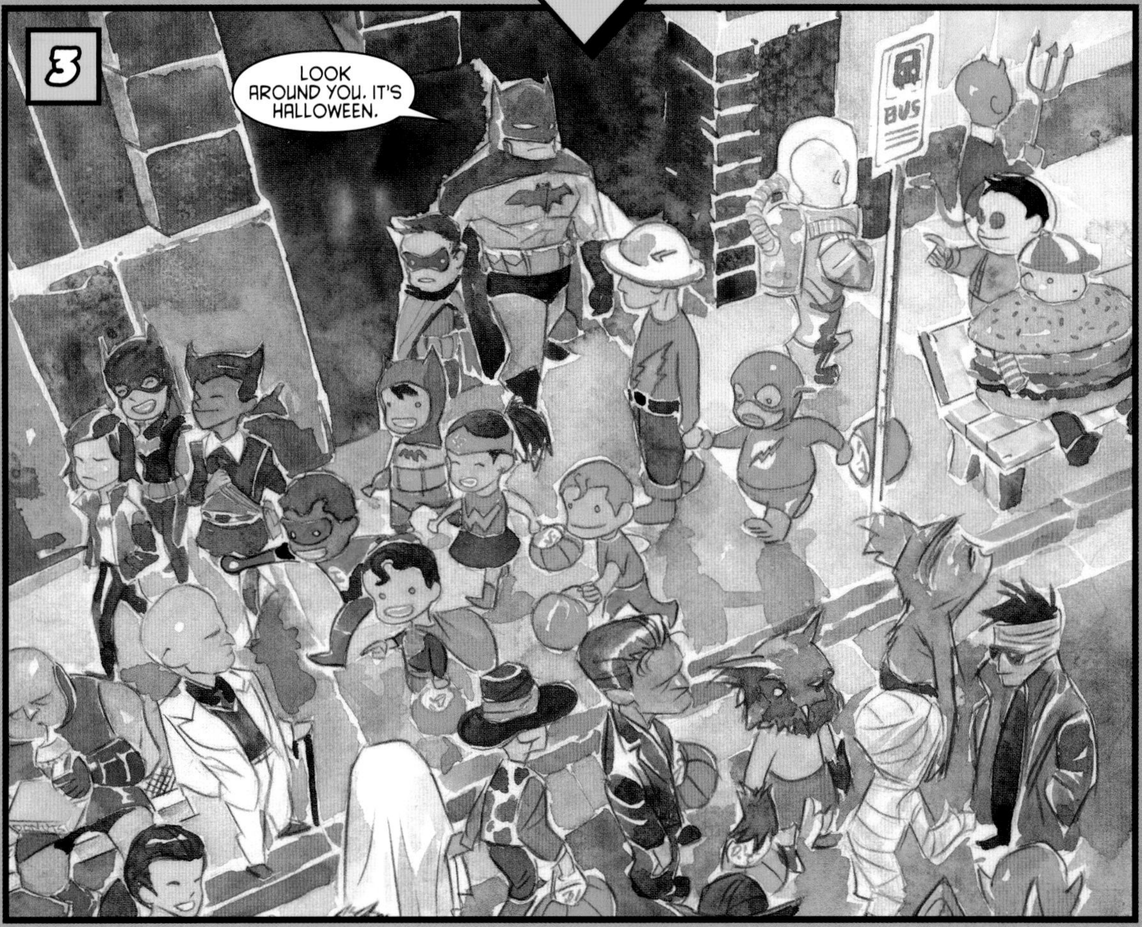
3
LOOK AROUND YOU. IT'S HALLOWEEN.
BUS

4. Why do some of the speech bubbles in this book have jagged edges? Explain your answer.

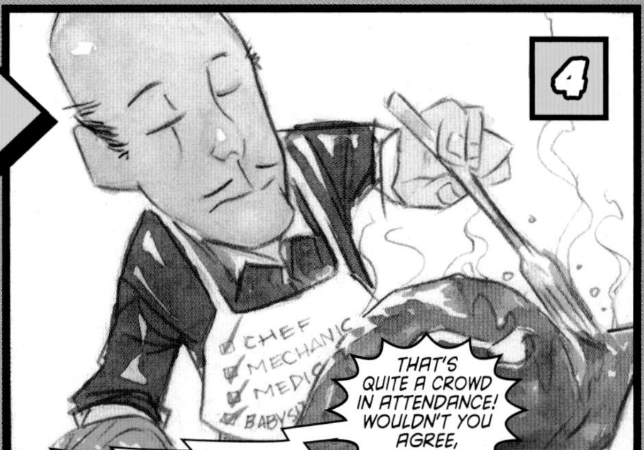
4
CHEF
MECHANIC
THAT'S QUITE A CROWD IN ATTENDANCE! WOULDN'T YOU AGREE, VICKI?

BATMAN™
LI'L GOTHAM

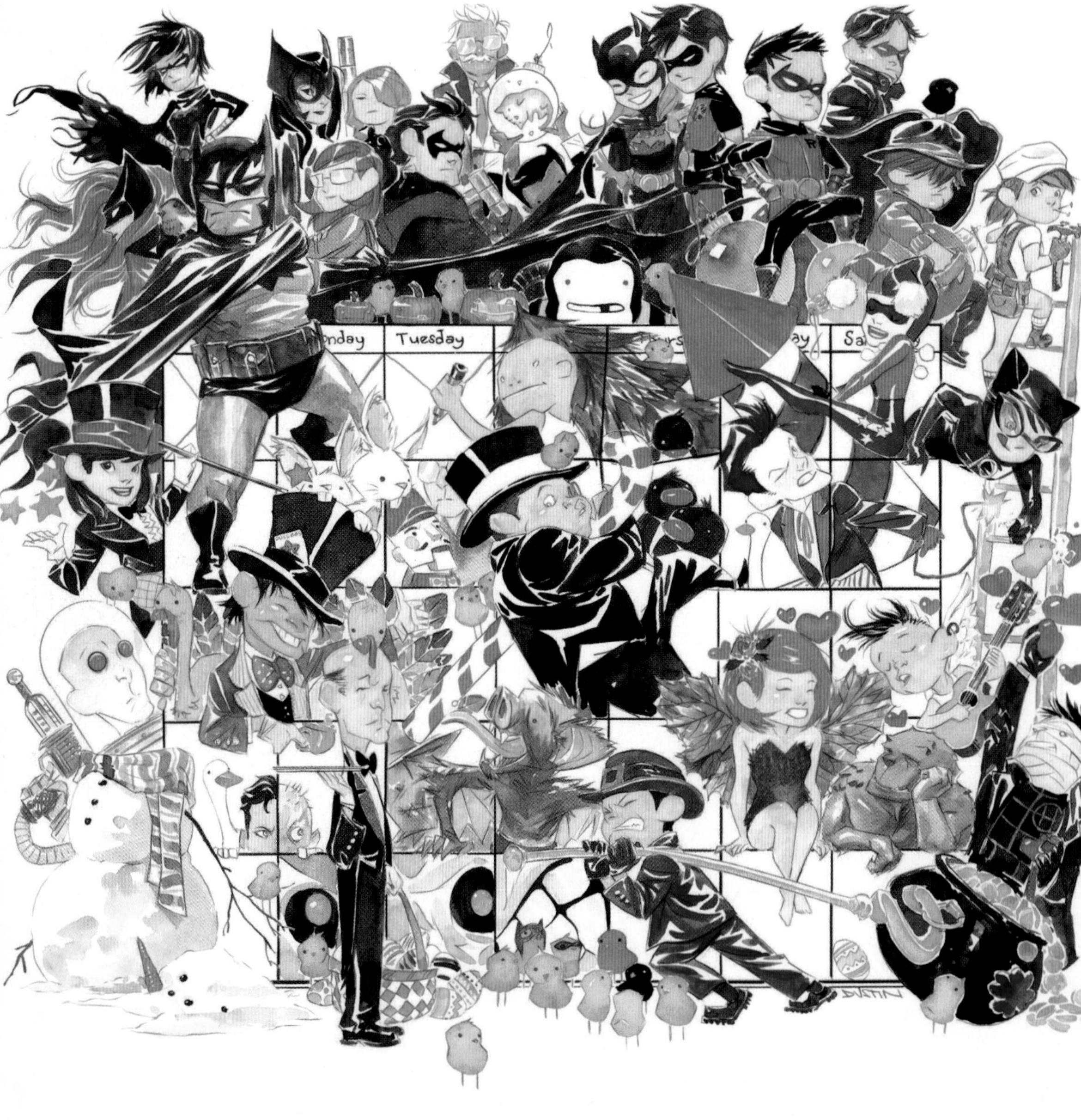
Tuesday

READ THEM ALL!

DC COMICS
BATMAN
LI'L GOTHAM
NGUYEN
FRIDOLFS
HALLOWEEN AND THANKSGIVING

DC COMICS
BATMAN
LI'L GOTHAM
CHRISTMAS AND NEW YEAR'S EVE
NGUYEN • FRIDOLFS

DC COMICS
BATMAN
LI'L GOTHAM
NGUYEN
FRIDOLFS
VALENTINE'S DAY AND THE LUNAR NEW YEAR

DC COMICS
BATMAN
LI'L GOTHAM
ST. PATRICK'S DAY AND EASTER
NGUYEN • FRIDOLFS

DC COMICS
BATMAN
LI'L GOTHAM
NGUYEN
FRIDOLFS
APRIL SHOWERS AND CINCO DE MAYO

DC COMICS
BATMAN
LI'L GOTHAM
NGUYEN
FRIDOLFS
MOTHER'S DAY AND FATHER'S DAY

only from...

STONE ARCH BOOKS™

a capstone imprint www.capstonepub.com

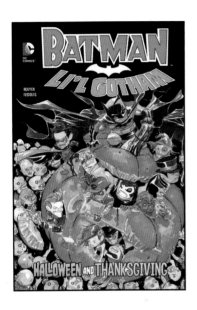

BATMAN™

LI'L GOTHAM

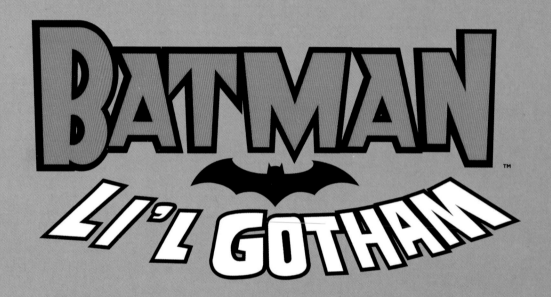